Apache Desert

Apache Desert
L. P. Holmes

Thorndike Press • Chivers Press
Waterville, Maine USA Bath, England

This Large Print edition is published by Thorndike Press, USA and by Chivers Press, England.

Published in 2001 in the U.S. by arrangement with Golden West Literary Agency.

Published in 2001 in the U.K. by arrangement with Golden West Literary Agency.

U.S. Hardcover 0-7862-3610-8 (Western Series Edition)
U.K. Hardcover 0-7540-4718-0 (Chivers Large Print)
U.K. Softcover 0-7540-4719-9 (Camden Large Print)

The text of this Large Print edition is unabridged.
Other aspects of the book may vary from the original edition.

Set in 16 pt. Plantin.

Printed in the United States on permanent paper.

British Library Cataloguing-in-Publication Data available

Library of Congress Cataloging-in-Publication Data

Holmes, L. P. (Llewellyn Perry), 1895–
    Apache Desert / L. P. Holmes.
      p. cm.
    ISBN 0-7862-3610-8 (lg. print : hc : alk. paper)
    1. Overland journeys to the Pacific — Fiction.
    2. Apache Indians — Wars — Fiction. 3. Large type
    books. I. Title.
PS3515.O4448 A85 2001
  813'.52—dc21   2001041565

CAST OF CHARACTERS

Steve Cloud, cashiered from the Army, was willing to risk his life to lead the train across the Apache desert.

Pete Orrick was more than just a mule wrangler, as he proved when Steve saved his life by pulling him from the river.

Col. Toyenbee knew Steve as one of the bravest of his officers — why didn't he speakup at the Courts-Martial?

Blake Ollinger was a handsome killer who wanted only one real chance to get at him, Steve knew.

Race Ellison was honest and square, his only trouble was he knew nothing of the desert, men or Apaches.

Lynn Ellison wanted desperately for their train to make good, but Steve Cloud's bruality shocked her.

1

Colonel Jason Toyenbee was a spare, hawk-faced man with silvering hair. In his office at Fort Yuma, where the air of the desert night lay hot and thick and breathless and the hanging lamp spread its light in a turgid yellow pool, he sat his chair with a sort of spraddled ease, his shoulders slack. Long years of cavalry duty in the desert had left him saddle leaned and leathery brown, and had put squint wrinkles at the corners of his shrewd, slightly tired eyes.

This same desert duty had given him other things, among them being an infinite wisdom concerning men and their ways, plus a generous breadth of judgment and a deep sense of elemental justice. He lighted a black cheroot and stabbed a forefinger at the pile of papers on the desk before him. There was a combative growl in his voice.

"As soon as I got word of the court-martial I sent to Crittenden at Bowie for a transcript of the findings. It didn't then and it doesn't now make sense to me that Lieu-

7

tenant Stephen Cloud could ever show the white feather. For I'd soldiered with that boy and I knew him thoroughly. I sensed something sour about the whole affair — and I was right. These findings are as full of holes as a sieve. Why, damn it, son, you seem to have put up no defense at all, and let that pompous jackass, Matlock, virtually ride you right out of the service. Even now, if you'll agree to putting up a fight, we can still rip this thing wide open. What's the matter — don't you want your name cleared?"

Stephen Cloud, ex-lieutenant of United States Cavalry, shrugged. "It's over and done with, sir. I prefer it left that way. I did not come here to ask you to intercede in my behalf. I came just to pay my respects and say good-by."

Colonel Toyenbee leaned back in his chair and through the curling smoke of his cheroot fixed Cloud with a stern but kindly scrutiny. He was looking at a man still a year shy of thirty, a man who made a tall and wiry figure, with saddle-narrowed flanks and good shoulders. He saw a long, clean-angled jaw, and, under thick dark hair and brows, eyes that were gray and reserved and slightly bitter.

A fine-looking lad, mused the colonel,

burned by desert wind and sun to a tan so deep as to be almost swarthy. And walled about now by a taciturn aloofness, a bitter withdrawing. That wall of reserve and the bleak shadowing about the eyes hadn't been there when this young officer had ridden under the colonel's command, three years before. Then there had been an open and fiery eagerness for life and all that it held that had attracted the older man.

For in it he had seen a reflection of his own youth and all the heady buoyancy those distant years had held, before time and the desert and all the accumulated vagaries of a man's fate and destiny moved in gradually to shrivel and quench the bright flame. The colonel cleared his throat.

"In the same packet of mail that brought this transcript of the court-martial findings was an announcement of the marriage of Captain Ellis Matlock to Miss Hetty Blair. You knew of that, Cloud?"

This was a deliberate and calculated probe at what the colonel suspected would be a raw wound. If he got the reaction he anticipated, then he would be provided with an answer not contained in the court-martial transcript.

He got the reaction all right. It came in the thinning of Steve Cloud's lips, in the unconscious clenching of his hands, and in low, almost toneless words. "I knew of that, sir."

Colonel Toyenbee sighed deeply, searched for a match to freshen his cheroot. He remembered Hetty Blair. A yellow-haired little slip, pretty, gay, and with a spark of deviltry in her eyes calculated to upset completely the emotional equilibrium of any normal young officer stationed in some far desert post where women were few and the loneliness of bachelor quarters could become a dreary thing.

Not, mused the colonel, that the girl had been in any way light. Perhaps a trifle flighty, but at the same time entirely shrewd enough to be fully cognizant of the advantages of a captain's rank and pay over that of a lieutenant's. And, frankly, not worth the messing up of a good man's career.

The colonel stood up, moved around the desk, and dropped a hand on Steve Cloud's shoulder. "Mighty good of you, son, to come this far to say hello and good-by. I appreciate it. I'm remembering those days when we soldiered together out of Fort Howiston. I'm remembering one night in particular in the Pinaleno Mountains. There was a thin dozen of us, while there was a Chiricahua Apache behind every

10

rock. That was a long night, wasn't it? But a good one in the memory of a soldier. And you, son, were a fine soldier, a damn fine soldier. The Army will be the poorer for having lost you. Any immediate plans?"

"Nothing in particular, sir. I'm going upriver on the *Spartan* in the morning. Good-by, sir. And thanks for everything."

Their hands met in a quick, hard gripping, and the colonel's free hand, still on Steve Cloud's shoulder, tightened and gave a little shake. Then the colonel turned to his orderly and said gruffly, "I'll see that Ellison girl now, Sergeant."

Steve Cloud passed the girl as she came in from the orderly room. He glimpsed her as a lithe, quick-striding figure with a pair of clear, level eyes which touched him briefly as she passed.

Outside, the night was warm and velvet black. It was breathlessly still, and across it lay the accumulated odors of the army reservation and the straggling town beyond and the musty, murky breath of the river. Steve Cloud went down to the river, pausing on the short wharf to which was moored the *Spartan*, paddle-wheel river boat.

Yonder was the river, rolling to the sea. The old Colorado, murky with the silt of half-a-dozen states, sullen and muttering and with a wild ferocity eternally in its heart. A hungry river, with no mercy in it anywhere. Never resting, or giving rest to anything which floated upon it. It sucked and gurgled at the pilings of the wharf and filled the *Spartan* with a vague unease, and the boat creaked and murmured and tugged endlessly at the mooring hawsers.

Steve Cloud prowled across the gang-plank and into the darkened bulk of the boat. He climbed to the texas deck and sprawled on the thin pallet of blankets spread there, his face to the stars. His thoughts ran far.

Now he felt that all ties with the past had been completely severed. This final and just-concluded visit with Colonel Toyenbee had marked the dividing line between the old and the new. He had, as the colonel had understood, come a long way to say good-by to a former commanding officer. But it had been something he wanted to do because, of all the men he had soldiered with, it was Colonel Toyenbee's opinion that he valued most.

Somehow he had known that his court-martial wouldn't matter in that fine old soldier's opinion; somehow he had known that Colonel Toyenbee would understand and hold him blameless. He had wanted that opinion — and needed it. He had needed it to bolster up his own faith in himself. Now that he had it he felt an ease of mind and spirit he had not known since those final bleak days at Bowie.

So it was a new trail, leading — where? It didn't particularly matter. The world was big and he was young. The past? Well, he wasn't going to drag that along with him forever, to be held down and bound by it. What was done, was done. He had made his own decisions for his own purpose. He had played the game the way he felt it should be played. If he had been overgenerous to someone who didn't deserve it, at least he'd been generous. He was at peace with himself. And so he slept.

The night ran its course and the stars blazed and faded and dawn light came in across the desert and lifted the river and the frontier post that was Fort Yuma out of the warm darkness. It cleared up the vague tangle that was the top hamper of the *Spartan* and etched the stanch little river boat into sharper detail. The faint, hissing whisper of exhaust steam that had grown in persistency for the past hour was now abruptly lost in a white plume shooting up beside the *Spartan*'s stack, and the whistle whooped in deep resonance.

Steve Cloud stood up, yawned, and stretched, blinking in the dawn light which now held the quality of hot gray steel. Thin mists coiled above the sliding river waters, filtered upward, and dissolved into nothingness. Full day approached rapidly, but this desert world seemed reluctant to accept it, for with day would come the sun with its long hours of blistering heat.

Ingrained habit could be persistently assertive in a man. From the meager sack of possessions that had been his pillow Steve Cloud dug out razor and soap, a small mirror, and a towel. From the half-breed cook in the galley he wangled a small pannikin of lukewarm water. He propped up the mirror, lathered his face and shaved, then made frugal ablutions. He took his breakfast from the cook and ate it standing by the galley door, coffee and bacon and tack.

The rumble of the *Spartan*'s whistle had brought Fort Yuma alive with a rush. A company of cavalry, afoot now, but destined as replacements for some distant back-country military post along the wild Arizona frontier, came marching down to the wharf, barrack bags on their shoulders. Following the military was a miscellany of other river travelers.

There were miners bound for Ehrenberg

14

and Quartzite and for the newly opened camp of Gold Road, far up the river. There were prospectors, bound only for their lonely and patient wanderings through the dangers and across the trackless miles of a country still new and young and raw. There were traders and merchants of one sort or another. There were black-frocked, nimble-fingered knights of the poker table and faro layout. There were drifters and doers, men of stanch purpose and men of no purpose at all. And all of them the *Spartan* took aboard and found room for.

Swooping down from the *Spartan*'s hog post, a stout manila hawser curved to meet the towing bridle of a barge that swung astern. The barge was fenced high and strongly except for a narrow gateway on the inboard side. A walled gangplank bridged the gap between this gate and the shore. Now came a long line of mules, led two by two by troopers from the fort. The animals were hustled across the gangplank on to the barge. Soon the barge was crowded with the animals, the gate was closed and secured, and the gangplank drawn. The four-footed cargo showed some concern at first, but soon began munching at the racks of wild hay along either side of the barge, or drank at the two big water puncheons that stood in opposite corners of the enclosure.

The *Spartan*'s whistle blared for a second time, and the influx of passengers quickened. Watching idly, Steve Cloud glimpsed the girl he had seen in Colonel Toyenbee's office the night before. Beside her, an attentive hand at her elbow, strode a man in gray flannel shirt and corduroy trousers tucked into the flat-heeled, broad-toed boots of a teamster. He had big shoulders and a mane of tawny hair that swept down from under a flat-crowned, wide-brimmed hat. As they closed in on the *Spartan*, the man said something which caused the girl to look up at him and smile. And there was a bright, clear beauty in that smile which even Steve Cloud, embittered as he was, did not miss.

A water-front loafer, frowzy and unclean, came lurching by. He also saw that smile, and he said something which made the girl recoil as though struck by a whip. Steve Cloud saw her face go white and her eyes blaze. Then the big man with her took a quick step forward and ripped over a smashing fist.

The river-rat tough went sprawling, but came back up, swift and snarling, the gleam of naked steel gripped in one hand. He carried the knife low and wide, ready for a ripping thrust as he gathered himself for a

16

forward lunge. And then the girl's companion, as coolly as he might have dealt with some mad animal, flipped a stubby-barreled derringer from a pocket and shot the tough dead in his tracks.

The report of the derringer was thin and flat, a sound like that of a distant whiplash. It awakened a lifting babble of voices and brought a pushing, shoving rush of the morbid and curious. The girl stood silent, shocked and white. But the big man with her seemed almost unconcerned. He stood looking down at the crumpled figure of the man he had killed while breaking his weapon, tossing aside the fired cartridge and replacing it with a loaded one. Then he pocketed the gun, took the girl's arm and drew her along.

For a third time the *Spartan*'s whistle thundered, and several Cocopa Indian deck hands made ready to ship the gangplank. A mooring hawser was thrown off and the *Spartan*'s bow began to swing with the current. There was a last moment of hurried rushing. Then the gangplank was shipped and the stern hawser dropped. A quiver ran through the *Spartan*. Steam hissed, and the big stern paddle wheel stirred and creaked and began its splashing beat. The *Spartan* gathered way, nosed aside the sullen river

17

waters, and thrust out toward midstream.

The towing hawser from the ship's hog post to the mule barge astern tightened and whined, and the barge eased into movement, sliding sideways before the thrust of the current until the control of the towing bridle took over, bringing the barge around, straightening it. The sighing of the *Spartan*'s exhaust took on a staccato beat. The wharf drifted back, the shore line began sliding away. Another upriver run had begun.

From his post on the texas deck Steve Cloud looked back. Fort Yuma seemed more barren and desolate than ever, now that the riverbank gaped empty. Empty except for a sprawled figure lying but a scant yard or two above the reach of the slimy river mud, with a few of those morbidly curious still standing around to gaze and wonder. While all around spread the desert, the everlasting desert, with the great river cutting through it, highway and highroad of many a man's dreams and hopes. Or the gulf of his despair.

Abruptly Steve Cloud turned his back on Fort Yuma. It was a significant move, for it meant that he was turning his back on all the past, washing out all of the high hopes and dreams he had once known, putting aside the exact scheduling of his blasted military career. That was done with. Ahead lay a new trail, neither plotted nor defined. Where it might lead he had no idea, nor at this moment felt that he greatly cared.

By the time the *Spartan* had reached midstream and was fully straightened out and committed to her upriver run, the rush was on for breakfast. Down on the cargo deck the Army had its own mess, but for the rest of the passengers the *Spartan*'s tiny galley, with its half-breed cook and helper, had to suffice. Which meant considerable waiting and somewhat rough service for the morning meal. Steve Cloud, having already eaten, was thankfully clear of all this.

The brassy sun had climbed into view and immediately its heat was a bitter power. Steve Cloud sought out a block of shade in the lee of the pilothouse and squatted there on his heels. Patience dropped over him like a cloak. It was the habit of long experience with the desert and its ways. It was a lesson a man had to learn if he was to exist in this country. For there was no hurrying of the desert or of the river, or of the endless march of the sun by day and that of the moon amid stars at night. Time was definite, distance was definite, established and immutable. A man molded his ways to these

19

established things, accepted their authority, or broke his heart fighting uselessly against them.

The impassive-faced Cocopa Indian who stood at the *Spartan*'s wheel in the pilot-house at Steve Cloud's back knew all these things. He was stoic and set for the interminable miles ahead, black eyes fixed on the yellow waters beyond the *Spartan*'s blunt and thrusting bow, giving a spoke or two of the wheel here, taking a spoke or two there, feeling his way through this flowing river's might that was ever surly and reluctant, ever hostile and treacherous.

Steve Cloud was so deeply immersed in his own locked-away isolation that he was unaware of the approach of the girl, of her big-shouldered, long-haired escort, and Captain Estee, the *Spartan*'s skipper, until they stopped right before him. Captain Estee, a stocky, barrel-chested man with a leathery face and squinty blue eyes, said, "Here's your man, Miss Ellison."

Steve stood up, trying, without too much success, to mask the annoyance he felt. Just now he was in no mood to meet strangers, least of all a strange woman. He looked down into eyes that were a clear hazel, bright and steady, businesslike, yet brushed with just a trace of shyness.

"You are — Stephen Cloud?" she asked.

Steve nodded briefly. "That's right."

"I am Lynn Ellison. Colonel Toyenbee suggested I give you — this."

She held out a folded note. Wondering, Steve took it. It was brief and to the point:

Suggest you have a talk with the bearer of this and listen well to her proposition. Last night she asked me if I could recommend a man of certain qualifications who might be open to hire. I immediately thought of you, for the qualifications fit you perfectly. Don't be too hasty in saying no, son. For you need something like this to keep your thoughts healthy. Remember, you're heading for a new start and there may be real opportunity behind this. Think on it.

The note ended with regards and Colonel Jason Toyenbee's sprawling signature.

The bitterness which had been simmering in Steve Cloud through the past many weeks began thrusting to the fore. Not so very long ago he had been an officer in the United States Cavalry. Subject to orders from a few superiors, but at the same time being in command of other men. Responsible for the men under him, for their welfare and conduct in the barracks and in the field.

Leading them in savage frontier battle with the Apache. A man's work in a man's world. Now here, it seemed, was something suggesting he go to work — for a woman, a young one, scarcely out of girlhood. Could any man's fortunes drop so far in so short a time?

The girl glimpsed the dark pride sweeping through his eyes and spoke swiftly, trying to head off the negative answer she saw forming. "I'm sure that if you'd let me explain the proposition, Mr. Cloud, we could come to a satisfactory agreement."

Her hair was auburn, silken soft, giving off coppery glints where the sun touched it. Her skin was faultless, soft tanned, her mouth and chin expressive. Well, he could remember another like her, with silken soft hair and skin so smoothly sun richened . . .

The man with the big shoulders spoke curtly. "Miss Ellison is waiting for an answer, mister!"

Steve Cloud turned the frowning intentness of his glance on the speaker. Captain Estee, a trifle hurriedly, said, "Meet Blake Ollinger, Cloud."

"I've seen Mister Ollinger before," said Steve coldly. "You still kill easily, don't you, Ollinger? Like back there at Yuma this morning. And like the other affair that I re-

22

call. At Wickenburg, it was, where the victim's name was Turnbell — Jeff Turnbell."

This Blake Ollinger was a handsome man. His features were strong and clearly cut. But there was a strangeness about his eyes. Cougar pale they were. And they had the cougar trick of going blank and moiling when their owner was startled.

They went that way now as Ollinger stared at Steve Cloud. Then his lips pulled thin in a smile that was without mirth. He spoke with a certain mocking ease.

"Now that you mention it, I recall the occasion. Wickenburg it was. You had a troop of cavalry quartered there for the night. And there was a poker game. This fellow Turnbell took his poker seriously, very seriously indeed. He just couldn't stand losing without wanting to shoot somebody. Me in particular. Quite naturally I objected, as any other sane person would. I had no choice in the matter if I wanted to go on living — which I did. As for that little affair back at Yuma, the ultimate proposition was the same. What would you have had me do, beg the tough's pardon? And him with a knife in his hand? That isn't the way of the river, Cloud."

"So it would seem," was Steve's curt retort. He swung his glance back to the girl.

"I'm sorry, Miss Ellison, but I'm really not interested. I have — other plans."

This was closing her out pretty bluntly, and her nod was stiff. "Of course. Thank you just the same."

She turned and went off along the deck. Blake Ollinger spoke to Captain Estee. "I'll take her breakfast to her." But instead of following the girl immediately, Ollinger turned to Steve again. "This Jeff Turnbell was a friend of yours, Cloud?"

"Jeff Turnbell was one of the best civilian scouts that ever matched wits with the Apache," said Steve. "We saw a lot of service together. Which made him more than a friend."

Blake Ollinger shrugged, his lips pulled thin again in that hard smile. "Which means that you probably don't like me. Well, as I said, that Wickenburg affair was an even shake. Turnbell was going for his weapon. And when any man goes to pull a gun or a knife on me, he wants to make damn well sure that he gets there first if he hopes to dandle grandchildren on his knee."

There was a challenging emphasis behind Ollinger's words and tone, a certain swaggering in his manner that rasped rawly across Steve Cloud's sensibilities. Grimness pulled at Steve's face.

"Should I ever have occasion to remember that, Ollinger, you can be sure I'll bear it in mind."

"Do that," mocked Ollinger. "The results could be interesting."

Ollinger turned away and headed for the galley. Captain Estee let out a sigh of relief and went off about his business.

Left alone, Steve Cloud dropped back into his former position, brooding. He knew a slight feeling of guilt over his abruptness with Lynn Ellison. It wouldn't have hurt to have listened to her proposition and he could have cushioned his refusal a little more tactfully. He still held the note Colonel Toyenbee had sent, and now he read it over again before crumpling it up in his hand.

The colonel's intentions had been well meant and kindly. At the same time, no one but himself could understand the restlessness that was in him, the desire to move and keep on moving, to get as far away from old associations and contacts as possible. In time, perhaps, he'd shake loose from this mood and be ready to settle down to a job of some sort. But at this moment, with a fair stake of money tucked away in his blanket roll, he had no other desire but to drift and keep on drifting.

The sun climbed higher, driving all shade from the weather deck of the *Spartan*. Steve Cloud went down to the cargo deck. It was hot down there, too, but at least there was shade. Men lolled here and there at what ease they could find, with the cavalry unit pulled off to one side by themselves, trading desultory banter. Looking at them, a faint shadow of commiseration showed in Steve Cloud's eyes.

Most of these troopers were comparative youngsters, freshly in from some eastern or midwestern post. Fed up with the hot and ugly monotony of Fort Yuma, they were eager for any change. While still lacking his thirtieth birthday, Steve Cloud had several years of desert experience behind him, and he felt infinitely old alongside of some of these downy-cheeked kids.

They had, he mused, little idea of what lay ahead of them. Some of those far, lonely posts along the Arizona frontier were little better than the thresholds of hell. There would these troopers find real monotony and blasting, relentless heat. And when they went out on campaign duty, why, then there would be the Apache waiting for them, the Chiricahua, the Mescalero, the Jicarilla.

So some of these troopers the sun and the desert would get, and some would fall to the

Apache. While those who lived would return much older than their years, with their gay and ruddy-cheeked youth left far behind them. For that was the way of the desert and the sun and the Apache with men who dared challenge them.

Looking for a reasonably quiet corner where he might rest, Steve moved past the idle troopers. Abruptly a booted foot pushed out, nearly tripping him up. The move had been deliberate, and Steve turned and stared down into scowling eyes and a heavy-featured, coarse face. The trooper was one of the few older ones and a man whom Steve now sharply remembered.

"Well, Loney," he said, "another hitch, I see. The wonder is that they never hung you long ago."

"What makes you so damned proud?" growled the trooper. "I heard about the court-martial. A coward they proved you, running out on a supply train you were supposed to guard, and letting the Apache have his way with every man jack on the wagons. So they took the bars off you and kicked you out, which brings you right down to the size where I can get at you, something I damn well yearned to do more than once in the past. So right here and now I'm going to beat the everlasting hell out of you!"

Loney was getting to his feet as he spoke. The moment he was fully erect, Steve Cloud caught him by the slack of his shirt, jerked him close, and hit him three times, short, wicked clubbing blows. Then he dropped him. Trooper Loney lay senseless, bleeding at the mouth.

Some of the other troopers, youngsters, started up, ready to take on Loney's quarrel, seeing in Steve Cloud just another civilian who had hit a soldier. But a voice of harsh authority stopped them short, and another of the old-timers, grizzled, and with a sergeant's stripes on his sleeve, stepped forward.

"Let be!" he growled. "Loney started this. It ain't the first time his big mouth has earned him a punch on the jaw. As you were!"

Steve Cloud turned away, his gray eyes almost black with anger and bitterness. And over there, where they had heard and seen the whole thing, stood the Ellison girl and her companion, Blake Ollinger. There was something in Lynn Ellison's glance which brought Steve's head up, his shoulders back, and his face a mask of bleak challenge. On Blake Ollinger's lips that thinly mocking smile formed and grew. Steve stepped over to him.

"You find things amusing, Ollinger?"

Ollinger shrugged, that maddening smile still working. "Interesting would be the better word. Particularly the spoken word."

Steve Cloud was all acrawl with the furious desire to give Ollinger some of the same treatment Loney had taken, to knock all the taunt and mockery out of him. But a man does not immediately shed the effects of long years of discipline and self-control. It might have been different if the girl hadn't been there. But she was there, almost within arm's reach, and that made a difference.

Steve turned and moved away, found the corner he was searching for and crept into it. Not unlike, he told himself morosely, a wounded animal seeking solitude.

This very thing which had jumped at him from the lips of Trooper Loney could, Steve realized now, always be a shadow at his shoulder. It was something he had not considered at the time of his court-martial. But, even if he had thought of it, things would have been no different. He'd still have kept his mouth shut and let Captain Ellis Matlock damn him utterly with his glib lies.

Steve had made his decision the morning he had faced the court-martial board in that barren, hot, cheerless room, with Colonel Crittenden presiding. Now he would have to abide by it, no matter what the future course. No one would ever thank him for what he had done, not even the girl he had done it for, Hetty Blair. For Hetty would never know. By this time she was married to Ellis Matlock, and certainly Matlock would keep the truth of his perfidy from her. Which seemed to put a period to the whole affair as far as Steve Cloud was concerned.

Aft sounded the steady, rumbling beat of the paddle wheel. Up forward, at regular intervals, echoed the cry of the Cocopa Indian deck hand who stood at the *Spartan*'s blunt bow, sounding the channel with a long pole, alert for some newly formed sand bar or for a submerged and treacherous snag, and calling his findings back to the pilothouse.

Driven by one force, guided by another, the *Spartan* plodded and pounded out her tenacious, stubborn way, constantly at battle with a third force, which was the turgid, sullen, never-relenting current.

This was the river trail.

2

One by one the *Spartan* touched various river towns and camps. Picacho, Cibola, Dent's Landing. Desolate, lonely, ugly little scatterings of gray buildings, crouched just above the mud line of the river, or huddled back along some low bluff that overlooked the swirling, silt-clogged waters. At each of them the *Spartan* left some of her varied passengers and some portion of her cargo.

The days and nights were a monotonous, unchanging pattern, beating out slow miles by day, laying up for the night in some steaming backwater, or moored to the rough landing of a rough town. For no skipper in his right mind would attempt a night run on this river, what with the ever-changing channels and the hidden snags lying in wait to tear the bottom out of an unwary craft.

Nor would the Cocopa Indian crew have anything to do with the river after dark, knowing their own superstitions concerning it and the demons it spawned in its dank and shadowy mists. The crew cleared out at

31

night and did their sleeping on shore.

The evenings were the toughest on Steve Cloud, that interval which lay between the movement and action of the day and the time when a man could lay himself down on his blankets under the stars and find forgetfulness in sleep. There was a raw and savage beauty in these evenings. On either hand, beyond the sprawling river flats, the desert ran away and away, powder-blue and empty to where, in some far distance, nameless mountains thrust gaunt and barren shoulders into the cooling sky. It was a vast and hostile land, fit setting for such a murky, bitter old river as the Colorado.

Keeping entirely to himself and for lack of other items of interest, Steve Cloud spent considerable time observing the mules in the towed barge. In charge of the animals was a friendly, leathery little man named Pete Orrick, with ragged, bleached hair, terrier-bright eyes, a twangy voice, and an inclination toward easy garrulity, who traveled back and forth between boat and barge by means of a sliding pulley rig on the towing hawser, going down to the barge by gravity, coming back to the *Spartan* through the efforts of a couple of deck hands working at a pull rope.

Pete Orrick fed the mules from the crib of

wild hay on the flat afterdeck of the barge, renewing the supply at every stop. He kept the water puncheons filled by means of a bucket, lowered at rope end to the river. At regular intervals he moved among the mules, currying and brushing, forcing the animals to mill quietly around and so get some certain small amount of exercise.

At times, his duties taken care of, Pete Orrick would squat on his heels beside Steve Cloud, suck on a stubby pipe, and ramble on with easy, unquestioning friendliness. And Steve would listen, not minding at all, for he knew a liking for this cheerful little man, and the open comradeship offered was a welcome break in his self-imposed loneliness.

Among other things, Steve learned from Pete Orrick that the mules belonged to Lynn Ellison and her brother, and were destined for Calumet, a landing above Ehrenberg. The Ellisons, it seemed, had won a government contract for the freighting of supplies from Calumet to some of the far inland army posts. The mules would do the hauling of these supplies.

What he learned from Pete Orrick regarding the mules Steve had already partly guessed, for the girl, Lynn Ellison, came often to stand at the far after end of the texas deck, look down at the mules, and confer with Pete Orrick concerning their welfare. Most of the time Blake Ollinger accompanied her.

The girl ignored Steve Cloud completely, but Ollinger always managed a side glance or two, with that faint, mocking smile touching his lips. And this smile never failed to grate across Steve's sensibilities and leave him glowering darkly at the bleak distances.

He tried to tell himself that neither the girl's utter indifference to his existence nor Ollinger's sly mockery meant a thing to him, one way or another. But though he avoided both of them as much as possible, he could not dismiss either of them completely from his thoughts. For, he realized, when you were coming to hate a man utterly, you could not ignore him, and if you knew a secret admiration for a girl, then you could not be indifferent to her presence, either.

For she was admirable. Several times had Steve guardedly observed her when she would stand there above the churning, pounding paddle wheel, cup slim, brown hands about her mouth, and in her clear young voice call some word down to Pete Orrick on the barge. At these times he would see in her a clean and slender grace and a vitality that was cool and unquenchable despite the sun's solid, unrelenting heat.

It did no good for him to tell himself that after his bitter experience of the past women and their ways would forever be a closed book as far as he was concerned. Back at Fort Bowie, with his mixed-up emotions concerning Hetty Blair so fresh in his mind, he'd been sure that this would be so. But those days were already far away; the past was past, and the present was where a man lived, after all. The present and the future — particularly if he was young.

They tied up for another night at the camp of Pomo, and Steve was distastefully considering the necessity of another none-too-savory supper from the *Spartan*'s galley. Here, as well as in other ways, was a grinding monotony, and he knew a restless rebellion against it. He was brooding over this when Pete Orrick, four-footed charges secure for the night, came over to him.

"Pomo ain't much of a camp," said Pete, "but it's got one thing worth while — an old Mexican woman who can dish up some mighty good grub. And I'm hungry for some. What do you say, son?"

Steve dropped a hand on the little man's arm. "Pete, I think you've saved my life."

They went across the gangplank eagerly,

and Blake Ollinger watched them go. A little later Ollinger went ashore himself and drifted quietly into the thickening dusk that shrouded the place.

The Mexican woman was old and squat and wrinkled, but her black eyes shone with friendliness at sight of Pete Orrick, who talked easily with her in her native tongue. Her kitchen was small but neat and lighted only by a couple of flickering candles. But the food was plentiful and varied and tasty and Steve Cloud got outside of the best meal he'd had in long weeks. On leaving he paid generously for both Pete and himself and smiled away the voluble thanks of the old woman.

They took their time sauntering back to the landing. Night had come down fully, velvet black. Mists climbing out of the river and across the mud of its banks flavored the world with a musty dankness. But also down across the desert came a cleaner, finer odor, the breath of sun-cleansed space and the dry-sweet flavor of some distant cedar brake.

Steve Cloud turned his face to this invisible lure and his blood knew a quickening stir. In the aftermath of his bitterness at the conclusion of the court-martial at Fort Bowie he had vowed, among other things, that he was through with this Arizona country. But he knew now that this would never be. For when a man has put several of the most vital years of his life in a land that had known the finest heights of his dreams and the lowest depths of his despair, why, then, in some strange way, he had become welded to it more tightly than he dreamed. His thoughts drifted far away, over some of the better back trails. And then he was jerked rudely back to the immediate present by a growling voice from the darkness.

"There he is. Get him!"

They seemed to spring up out of the very earth's blackness — four of them. And more through sheer instinct than because he saw it coming, Steve Cloud dodged under the swing of a club. Thrown off balance by the force of his own effort, the wielder of the club stumbled into Steve, who automatically slugged the fellow in the body savagely and brought him bent over and gasping.

Steve grabbed him, got a hip under him, and threw him, hard! Steve was diving forward, knees bunched, when a fist bounced glancingly off the side of his head and a man's full weight drove heavily down upon his shoulders. The impact smashed Steve forward and down, but served a purpose the assailant had not figured on. For it gave twice the power and wicked drive to Steve's bunched knees when they dug into the body of the fellow who had swung the club.

Under his knees Steve felt ribs spring and collapse, and the man on the ground let out a hoarse bawl of agony. And the one who had leaped on Steve's back, with Steve hunched and falling away under him, slid on over the round of Steve's shoulders and hit face down and floundering on the dark earth beyond.

Steve knew what he wanted. That club! He got a hand on it, tore it from a grip gone loose and weak, then surged back to his feet, whirling.

"Pete!" he yelled. "Pete — !"

Pete Orrick's muffled, desperate answer came up from the earth, for two of the roughs had put Pete down with that first rush and now were working at him with their boots.

"Kickin' me — Steve! Damn cowards — !"

Steve swung the club in a sideways sweep. It thudded solidly home and the bone in a rough's arm cracked under the weight of it. The rough spun away into the blackness, cursing thinly. His companion left off kicking at Pete Orrick, drove at Steve, and the chopping club met him head on. He went down in a heap.

With his free hand Steve reached for Pete, hauled him to his feet, then whirled to face any further attack. There was none. The pound of running boots diminished in one direction. In another a thin cursing was fading. Steve Cloud headed on for the river and the *Spartan*, steering Pete Orrick's stumbling steps.

"We're getting out of here," he panted. "There may be more of them."

But they reached the gangplank with no further trouble. Steve Cloud, realizing he still carried the club, tossed it over the side. The *Spartan* was quiet. They climbed to the texas deck, Pete grunting a little from his bruises. The door of Captain Estee's cabin was open, letting out a thin flare of light, and showed Captain Estee there, talking to Lynn Ellison and Blake Ollinger. Pete Orrick's boots dragged a little, and at the sound the girl turned.

"Pete!" she called. "Is that you?"

"Yeah," mumbled Pete. "Me and Steve Cloud. Somethin' you wanted?"

"Nothing in particular. I was wondering where you were. You generally stay aboard."

"Steve an' me went ashore for a meal of different grub," explained Pete. As he spoke he moved close enough for the light to touch him. There was a little smear of blood seeping from one corner of his mouth. The girl exclaimed softly.

"Pete — you're hurt!"

"Some," agreed Pete, "but nothin' serious. Steve an' me were on our way back to the boat when some roughs jumped us. They had me down an' were set to kick my ribs in, but Steve showed 'em what for in one damn big hurry."

"These river towns!" growled Captain Estee. "They're pretty wild."

The girl moved up to Pete Orrick, dabbing gently at his battered mouth with a wisp of handkerchief. It was a swift, instinctive move, realized Steve Cloud, thoroughly indicative of this girl's fine make-up.

"But why," cried the girl, "would anyone be after you, Pete?"

"Dunno." The little man shrugged. "More likely they were after Steve, though I can't figger that, either."

Blake Ollinger spoke smoothly. "Lot of drifters along the river who are broke and down and out. They'd cut any man's throat for a dollar."

"It doesn't explain away that easy," said Steve Cloud harshly. "They were looking for a certain man. One of them said as much when they first charged in."

Ollinger shrugged, showing that faint

mockery again. "Could have been some of the military, Cloud. Maybe that fellow Loney wasn't the only one aching for a chance at you now the bars are off your shoulders."

There was, thought Steve bleakly, a chance that this might be so. Trooper Loney, as Steve remembered the man, had always been a malcontent, never a really good soldier. The man had always been a troublemaker, had seen plenty of guard-house confinement. He was the sort to harbor a grudge forever and overlook no chance at satisfying it. He could have talked some of the other younger and more impressionable troopers into this ring.

Steve went off without another word to stretch out on his blankets and think about it. But a little while later he went down to the cargo deck and there sought out the gruff sergeant in charge of the troops.

"Any of your men go ashore this evening, Sergeant?"

"Not any," was the reply. "Most of the lads I could trust, but there's a few, such as that fellow Loney, who might never come back if I let 'em beyond my sight. So, to play safe, they stay on this boat until it's time to leave it for good. Why do you ask?"

"Just a little affair of personal interest," evaded Cloud. "Thanks a lot, Sergeant."

When Cloud got back to his blankets he found Pete Orrick squatted down beside them, smoking. "I been tryin' to figger it," mumbled Pete. "But I can't get no good answer. Like you told Ollinger, those roughs were after a certain man. I heard 'em give that yell when they come bargin' in. It couldn't have been me they wanted. I don't amount to enough any way you take me to make a bunch of river roughs gang me. It must have been you, Steve, who they wanted. Mebbe Ollinger's right — mebbe it was some of them sogers."

Steve Cloud shook his head. "Not any of them, Pete. I just talked to the sergeant in charge and he said none of them left the boat. No, the military had nothing to do with it."

Pete Orrick probed some sore ribs with a careful forefinger. "Well, anyhow, we come out of it with whole skins — which is somethin'. More'n one man has had a knife slipped into him an' then been rolled into the river an' never seen or heard of again. She's a wicked old river in more ways than one."

The next stop above Pomo was Ehrenberg, and here the military disembarked for their long trip inland. To Steve Cloud,

42

watching the cavalrymen file across the gangplank, this was indeed a final good-by to the old days. There was something very like wistfulness in Steve's eyes as he watched them. Then he resolutely turned his back. It was as he had told himself before: What was done — was done.

Also, at Ehrenberg, Blake Ollinger left the *Spartan.* From his vantage point beside the pilothouse Steve Cloud watched as Lynn Ellison said good-by to Ollinger. Maybe it was real, maybe it was imagination on Steve's part that their final handclasp was lingering, and he wondered why this fact irked him. Perhaps it was merely because Blake Ollinger was a man he never could like. The man was a powerful, confident, swaggering figure, colorful, good-looking. But Steve was remembering how Ollinger had struck with swift and deadly efficiency. Once at Wickenburg, when a civilian scout, Jeff Turnbell, had died under Ollinger's flashing gun and again back at Fort Yuma when a river rough had died the same way.

According to the accepted code of a rough and wild frontier, perhaps Ollinger had been justified in both cases, for Jeff Turnbell had been a savage fighter in his own right, and certainly the river tough at Yuma had pulled a knife. Yet there was a certain ruthlessness in Ollinger's actions that indexed him, and of one thing you could, realized Steve, be sure. If occasion warranted, Blake Ollinger could be a tough and unforgiving enemy. And a sly one, if that mockery which showed so much in his eyes was any indication.

As for himself, Steve still had no idea at what landing he would leave the *Spartan*. He had no real plans and therefore no real destination. Of course he could always have gone home, back to the East. But this was out of the picture. Back there, among old friends and associations, he would have much explaining to do about something for which there was no explanation except to himself.

Besides, having once tasted the virile, restless life of this frontier, he knew he'd never again be satisfied with more settled and prosaic surroundings. The spell of this country was in his blood now and would never leave him.

He remembered a stretch of country he'd once traveled through while on patrol. Piñon country it was, a land of blue-green timber that opened into little parks rich in graze; a country high enough so that the air was tempered with a certain crispness and where the breath of the very trees lay rich and aromatic. And he remembered one of the troopers — a lank Texan corporal it was — remarking that here was good cattle country. Maybe that was what he was looking for, a cattle ranch in the piñon country. It would be a rough, hard life with plenty of obstacles in the way, but it would be a man's life.

Certainly, Steve decided, he wanted no part of mining. To grub in the earth after the metallic treasures it held was in no way luring to him. He wanted more freedom than that, with a good horse between his legs and wide miles to ride in.

He had heard some talk of a new camp far up in the great canyon of the Colorado, where the Virgin River came down. A wilderness trading post it was, with pack trains running out of it through southeastern Nevada and even up into Utah. A job at that sort of work would mean plenty of riding and far trails to cover. And in that country he certainly would have no trouble in losing himself from all past associations. . . .

Ehrenberg was a day and a half's travel down river. All around the world was empty and seemingly without life of any sort except that which the *Spartan* contained, and the spirit of the eternal river. And Steve Cloud thought that a man could not travel this river day after day without beginning to wonder if perhaps the Cocopa Indians weren't right, after all, in their contention that the Colorado had a demon heart and was constantly on the watch for a chance to snatch at and swallow up the unwary.

Since leaving Ehrenberg, Steve had seen Lynn Ellison several times, but, as before, she ignored him, and it seemed to Steve that in her cool unconcern he could sense something almost like contempt. And he wondered about this. Just because he had refused to go to work for her was no occasion for her feeling that way toward him. Unless, somehow, she had heard the story of the Fort Bowie court-martial, with the inevitable inferences such a telling would always lend to the affair.

Steve was thinking of this as he stood in the full drive of the sun, with the dank, wet smell of paddle-foamed water lifting to him. Down on the barge Pete Orrick was busy at his chore of tending the mules. At the moment Pete was forking wild hay into the feed racks. A brisk step sounded at Steve's side, and there stood the girl he'd been musing about. As always, despite the heat, she was crisp and fresh and cool-looking. Steve thought she meant to speak to him, and he touched his hat and murmured a greeting.

But she was intent on other things, and for all the concern she showed, Steve Cloud simply did not exist. She cupped her hands about her mouth and called an order down to Pete Orrick.

Pete, with a forkful of hay balanced over one shoulder, was treading a careful way along the narrow catwalk above the feed racks. When the girl's call reached him, he looked up and turned, and then began to waver, caught off balance by his own move and the sagging weight of that forkful of hay.

Pete twisted desperately, trying to save both himself and the forkful of hay. He saved neither, and when he fell it was so suddenly done as to seem almost deliberate. The hay went into the river and Pete followed, striking the fender of the barge as he dropped. Steve Cloud saw the garrulous, likeable old fellow's head slap against the fender and saw also the utter limpness of limb and leg and body as the brown water reached up hungrily to suck old Pete down.

The girl's broken cry was only a far-off echo of sound to Steve, for almost before Pete hit the water Steve was yanking off his boots. He was really conscious of just one thing. Pete Orrick, knocked senseless as he fell, would never come out of that river alive — unless — !

Steve took two steps and dived, far and wide. The water rushed up at him with a savage impact. Then he went far, far down into the dark, dank depths of it. This was wicked water, hungry water, heavy and thick and charged with mud and silt. It had hidden, twisting currents in it that caught at a man and laid a dragging weight all across him, sluggish and gripping. It was water famed for never giving up what it once had full hold on.

Steve fought it with powerful strokes, driving for the surface, spinning around and around in the rolling eddies of the *Spartan*'s wake. His head broke clear, and he forced himself out as high as he could, gulping in another lungful of air and shaking the water from his eyes. He saw nothing about him but a battered sea of dirty foam and the stern of the barge a little to his left and drawing steadily upstream past him. Then he forgot all that as he searched for some sign of Pete Orrick.

He knew it would be useless to dive and try to find Pete under the water unless he had some idea of where to look. For that would be blind purpose in this opaque, silt-thickened medium. His only chance was that the turbulence set up by the *Spartan*'s paddle wheel might spin a senseless man to the surface for a brief second before sucking him under forever.

Again Steve drove himself as high above the surface as he could, his head swinging from side to side in frantic search. And then he saw it, a man's arm and shoulder lifting and rolling just inches above the foam before starting down again with a sickening finality.

Steve was a good twenty feet away. He drove for the spot with savage purpose, grabbed deep, and got nothing but empty water. He reared, porpoised, and dived deep, swimming with the current and sweeping searching hands blindly ahead to either side and below him.

He stayed down so long that a deadly pressure began to build up in his head and lungs. Yet he knew that if he took time to return to the surface again and get enough air into him for another dive, the river would have taken its prey beyond any thin hope of recovery. This had to be it — now!

He drove along for another half-dozen desperate strokes, going deeper, reaching, feeling, grabbing. And then, of a sudden, he got it, a handful of cloth, with the firmness of human flesh underneath. He changed course, fought for the surface. For air — air — !

He began to despair that he could do it. It seemed as though some fiendish demon had hold of this same senseless burden and was fighting him for possession of it, trying to drag it from his grasp and ever deeper into the black depths. Steve's heart was hammering in his breast like some caged and frantic thing, and the hunger for air in his straining lungs was a raw red agony. But also there swept through him now a sort of mad fury, a final all-out burst of desperation effort.

With his free hand he clawed at the river, kicked at it, forced himself upward, dragging Pete Orrick with him. Up — up, shaking the demon's grip loose. Up again, another clawing stroke, another kick. And then he'd done it. Air struck his dripping head and face — air! And he sucked it in with deep, shuddering gulps. The clear sky over him — the brassy glare of the sun, a glorious thing now, full of bright beauty. And clear air, to fill his lungs again and again, while his wild heart quieted and the savage pressure in his head dwindled and went away. He rolled over on his back and lifted Pete Orrick's face to the open air too.

For a little time he was content to drift so, swimming just enough to hold his own with that he had torn from the river demon's grip. For he had left so much in that blind and brutal battle in the depths, it took some time to get it back. It came, slowly at first, then with a renewing surge, and Steve set out to win the rest of this fight.

He was well over a hundred yards below the *Spartan* and the barge by this time, with the sweep of the current constantly increasing that distance. He knew he had no chance of regaining them against the current's wrath. Shore was his only chance, and the nearer one, over to his left, was a dishearteningly long way for even a strong swimmer with a senseless companion to support and tow. While the ever-hungry river never let up for an instant in its constant efforts to suck both men down again to oblivion. But a man did not go halfway to hell and fight a way back to drift down to such a dread end without a fight to the finish. Steve Cloud struck out for that distant shore, dragging his man with him.

Steve neither saw nor heard any of the excitement and momentary confusion aboard the *Spartan*, which slowed the beat of the paddle wheel until its thrust was just enough to hold the *Spartan* dead against the drive of the current. Nor the further haste with which a dinghy was being lowered overside, to be manned with none other

51

than Captain Estee at the oars, while Lynn Ellison crouched in the stern. All Steve saw and concentrated on was that shore line which drew gradually closer as he doggedly clawed his way on.

Strange and disjointed thoughts came to him. He remembered his first patrol against the Apache under that grim old soldier, Colonel Jason Toyenbee, and the briefing the colonel had given him and another junior officer.

". . . you'll know thirst until you'll think you cannot stand another minute of it — yet you'll put it behind you and go on. You'll know weariness that will eat at your heart and at your brain and drive you numb. But you'll master that too — and go on — and on — and — on — !"

The word kept beating through his mind like a cadence with which he measured each clawing stroke. On — and on — and — on — !

The shore came closer. It had to. Fifty yards away — twenty. And then the river demon made a last malignant try for its prey. Steve's steadily beating legs thrust into the tangling branches of a submerged snag, some ancient cottonwood, overpowered and claimed by the river, that had drifted down and anchored in some sodden bar of mud.

The branches of the snag seemed equipped with a thousand clutching fingers, gripping and clawing tenaciously. Steve Cloud fought them, cursed them, broke free of them, and struggled into the quiet water of an eddy. Here the river hid its wolfishness, turned almost benignant. Defeated this time, it would wait another chance.

Steve's clawing hand lost itself in the soft slime of mud. His legs beat through the same murky stuff. Then, like some half-dead animal, he was wallowing up a slope of it, half-crawling, half-lunging. But always dragging Pete Orrick with him. And finally there wasn't even any mud to fight through. There was land, solid land. And then, with a long, broken sigh, Steve Cloud flattened out and went still.

3

Steve did not hear the dinghy slide up on the bank beside him. He did not even know it was around. He knew nothing until Captain Estee gripped his shoulder and turned him over face to the sun, and called him in husky, anxious tones. Only then did Steve climb back out of the daze and apathy and lethargy of almost complete exhaustion.

His own voice sounded foreign to him, for it was just a mumbled croak.

"I'm all right — all right. Get busy on Pete. Get the water out of him. I don't know whether I brought a live man or a dead one out of that God-damned river — !"

The sun beat hot and strong and vital on his head and shoulders and the blaze of it made him close his eyes. What a tremendous thing it was to be able to rest — rest! To sag into complete stillness while the rasp of laboring breath eased in his throat and chest and the roaring pound of blood in his ears softened until he was once more conscious of small, individual sounds. One of these was a gasp and a liquid coughing and then the weak, nasal mutter of Pete Orrick's voice. Another was a deep growl of relief by Captain Estee. Steve sat up and looked around.

Captain Estee and Lynn Ellison had jackknifed Pete Orrick across a driftwood log to drain the water out of him. Now, with Pete stirring and mumbling, they eased him off this, and the girl, kneeling, supported Pete's head and shoulders. The girl was still very pale and her lips were trembling and her eyes were big and dark and shining with the tears of relief. Captain Estee turned to Steve Cloud.

"You brought a live one out, boy," he said gruffly. "Though I'm damned if I know how you did it. Twenty years I've been up and down this old hellion of a river and this is the first time I ever saw it give up a man it once had a real grip on. How you ever got nerve to go in after Pete, I can't understand. I could never have done it. The next person to tell me there's anything wrong with your courage has got an argument on their hands, right then and quick! How you feeling?"

"Good enough," answered Steve quietly. "You sure Pete's all right?"

"Sure he's all right. We poured about a gallon of river water out of him. He'll be a little peaked for a day or two, but nothing worse. Well, we might as well get out of here."

Captain Estee lifted Pete bodily into the dinghy and the girl crouched down on the floor boards of the little craft, cushioning Pete's head with her knee. Steve Cloud took his place in the stern and Captain Estee manned the oars and sent the dinghy driving out into the stream with powerful, expert strokes.

The *Spartan* was up there, waiting, holding her place against the current, and the dinghy nosed its way up to her and alongside. Members of the Cocopa Indian crew lent eager hands to help them aboard, and they looked at Steve Cloud with something almost like awe in their black eyes. For here was a man who had fought the river demon right in its very lair, and whipped it. They patted him on the back and murmured words he could not understand.

Captain Estee, observing, smiled grimly. "You've created a legend, Steve. Fifty years from now the Cocopa Indians will still be telling the story. They're not exactly sure whether it's really you or your clothed spirit that's come back out of the river."

"Not too sure myself," answered Steve. "I left a lot of energy out in that water."

They put Pete Orrick to bed in Captain Estee's own cabin and dosed him with a big shot of whisky. Pete, pawing weakly, got hold of Steve's hand. "Never will forget this, boy. I'd have been a gone rooster but for you."

"You shut up and go to sleep," growled Steve. "Don't fret yourself about the mules. I'll take care of them."

Steve had a change of clothes in his duffel bag. He got these, went down to the engine room, where he stripped and had a sweating Cocopa Indian deck hand sluice him off with several buckets of fresh water. Cleansed of the river mud and its smell, he dressed in dry clothes, and aside from a slight feeling of "goneness" in the pit of his stomach, felt his old self once more. Topside, he found an area of shade beside the pilothouse, lay down, and slept for an hour. After that he went down the sliding rig on the towing hawser and took over the chore of tending the mules.

That night the *Spartan* tied up at the mouth of a side lagoon. After he'd eaten supper Steve Cloud stopped at Captain Estee's cabin. Lynn Ellison was just coming out, closing the door very quietly behind her. Glimpsing Steve, she spoke softly.

"Pete's just gone to sleep again. But if you

want to see him — ?"

"No," murmured Steve. "Not necessary, I was just checking up."

He started to turn away, but found the girl beside him, a little hesitant. "Could — could I talk to you a moment, Mr. Cloud?"

"Of course. What is it?"

She was quiet while they walked back to stand above the now-silent paddle wheel. Steve got out his pipe, stoked it, and fired up. The stillness and the weird beauty of the desert night were all about them. The stars were the brightest of jewels, piercing a sky of black velvet. Here, at the mouth of this lagoon, even the river was still, and the *Spartan* lay completely inert, with none of the usual restless creakings and stirrings. The harsh croak of a night heron sounded once back along the lagoon somewhere, then the silence took over once more.

Steve Cloud said nothing, watching the girl guardedly. She was just a slim shadow beside him. Finally she spoke, with a certain shy impulsiveness.

"Tomorrow we will reach Calumet, where I will be leaving the *Spartan*. I was afraid I might not get another chance to apologize to you."

Steve was startled. "Apologize — to me! What for?"

"For things I have thought and things I have said about you that were very wrong. I listened to words against you that I shouldn't have. For they were wrong, very wrong. And I was guilty of repeating them. I'm sorry for that, and I do apologize. You are certainly not a coward, but instead a very brave man. I hope you'll forgive me."

Here, thought Steve, was that Fort Bowie story reaching after him. How far, he wondered with some bitterness, would he have to travel to get completely away from it? His answer was quiet.

"There is nothing to forgive, Miss Ellison. But I do appreciate your thought."

She was silent for another little time, then said, "I don't suppose you would reconsider my original offer — the matter that Colonel Toyenbee mentioned in his note?"

There was no use Steve trying to deny the warmth and uplift of spirit that these last few moments had given him. He had been sunk in an abyss of loneliness of spirit far deeper than he realized. He had felt like a virtual pariah in this girl's eyes, and the normal youth of him had rebelled strongly.

"It all had to do with some sort of a job, didn't it?" he asked.

"Yes. You see, my brother and I have been awarded a contract by the government to freight supplies in to some of their inland posts. We have the wagons, we have the mules. We have men to drive the wagons. But we have no one who really knows the back country well, or who understands the Apache and how to thwart them. We need such a man to take charge. Colonel Toyenbee recommended you."

"Miss Ellison," said Steve, "there is no such man. One who understands the Apache thoroughly enough to thwart them, I mean. If I learned nothing else during my tour of military duty, I learned that. Running a freight route through Apache country is about as dangerous a project as I can imagine, and to make a success of it you'll need unlimited luck and the blessing of God."

"Somebody has to attempt it," said the girl stoutly. "And it might as well be me and my brother, Race. It is our big opportunity, and if we can put it over it means assured success for the future. Besides, if you don't agree to take over, you will rob us of the services of another man we had counted on, a man who understands the care of mules better than any other."

Steve swung his head. "I don't understand. What man is that?"

"Pete Orrick. It's quite simple. When you

saved him from the river today you won yourself a faithful shadow who'll follow you all the rest of his life. Pete told me that himself not over half an hour ago. He said he didn't want to leave our employ, but if you went on upriver, then he was going upriver too."

The first real smile that had touched Steve Cloud's lips in long weeks now settled there. "But if I were to go to work for you, then Pete would stay on too. Is that it?"

"That's it."

Steve looked out across the night. Why not? Why not go to work for this girl and her brother? The first dark pride that had caused him to refuse her offer originally no longer burned so stubbornly. Time and the river had knocked a lot of that out of him. And, after all, he had to go to work somewhere, for somebody. Here was a chance for movement, for contact with the frontier he'd come to love. Here would be the challenging spice of hardship and danger. And perhaps, as Colonel Toyenbee had said in his note, here also might wait opportunity. Of a sudden his mind was made up.

"You won't lose Pete, Miss Ellison. I'll take that job. I hope I can do you some good at it."

She turned to him impulsively. "I'm very

61

glad, Stephen Cloud, I know we will both profit. Thank you!"

She touched his arm with the briefest of pressure, then hurried away.

When Steve Cloud lay down to sleep that night, he knew a contentment that had long been missing. The restless unease that had dogged him for so long was gone. He had been all at odds and ends, lost without the fixed order and routine of the military years. Now, once again, something definite lay ahead.

Shortly after noon of the following day the *Spartan* tied up at the landing of Calumet. The town itself stood on a low benchland some two hundred yards back from the river, sunbaked and dusty, but showing more life and vitality than most of the other camps the *Spartan* had stopped at. A sizable crowd had gathered at the landing and one of the foremost of these, a well-set-up young fellow of about Steve Cloud's age, came hurrying across the gangplank the moment it was run out.

Watching, Steve saw him give Lynn Ellison a brief hug and a peck on the cheek and heard him exclaim, "About time, sis. I been pawin' the ground. The mules all safe and sound? And no trouble? No sign of Fallon and Overgaard?"

"Not a sign, Race," answered the girl. "And no trouble at all. We've probably been imagining dangers that don't exist."

The young fellow shook his head. "We never imagined a thing. Probably the opposition figured it would be too difficult to pull a raid farther down the river and are just waiting a more favorable chance. Any luck in locating a wagon boss?"

"Yes. Come and meet him."

Race Ellison had a hard, firm handclasp and Steve Cloud liked him for that and for the directness of his eyes. But Race showed some surprise.

"I expected to see an older man, Cloud. You've had experience with the back country — and the Apache?"

"Quite a bit." Steve nodded. "I promise nothing, though, except my best."

"That's all any man can give." Race Ellison grinned. "Where's Pete Orrick?"

"In Captain Estee's cabin," explained the girl. "A little under the weather but coming along all right. There was an accident yesterday afternoon. Pete fell into the river and Mr. Cloud went in after him."

"You mean," exclaimed Race, amazed, "that Pete actually was in the river and that Cloud brought him out? That isn't supposed to happen in this river."

"I know." The girl nodded. "But it's still a fact. It was a rather tremendous thing."

Race looked Steve Cloud over again, a deepening respect in his eyes. "It must have been all of that. There's Pete now."

Looking somewhat peaked and moving slowly, Pete Orrick came across the deck to join them. The girl scolded him gently. "You're not supposed to be up and around, Pete. The *Spartan* will be tied up here until noon tomorrow and you should have stayed in your bunk until then. I thought I told you that."

"You did," agreed Pete. "But while I'm a mite frayed around the edges I ain't that bad off. Chores to do, Lynn — chores to do. Got to get the mules ashore an' corralled." He looked up at Steve Cloud. "Lynn tells me you're signin' on, boy. That's fine. I want to see this job through myself. We'll do it, you an' me."

Steve grinned down at the old fellow. "And you'll start taking orders now. The first one is that you take it easy and leave the unloading of the mules up to me."

"That's right," chimed in Race Ellison. "I got some skinners who been doing nothing else but lay around. High time they started earning their wages."

The corrals and the Ellison wagon camp

were above town at the inland edge of a sprawling river meadow. With the help of the several skinners who were to drive the wagons, Steve and Race Ellison got the mules unloaded from the barge and safely corralled. This chore done, Steve took the opportunity to look over the wagons. They were towering, high-wheeled, broad-tired Merivale desert wagons, with hickory bows and weathered canvas tops. They were in fine shape, virtually new, and, along with the mules and harness necessary, represented a considerable investment. Well, there was no use trying to tackle the desert and the back country with anything but the best.

Back at the landing, Captain Estee had his Cocopa Indian deck hands and several town idlers who wanted to earn a dollar or two working busily unloading a pile of cargo — supplies in boxes and bales and kegs — all carrying the United States Army quartermaster stamp on it. Vital stuff this, destined for another lonely cavalry post somewhere in the wild interior, and Steve Cloud, coming back from the corrals, watched the work soberly.

Many had been the times when he had ridden in escort of wagon trains of such supplies through hostile Apache country, and well he knew the vital importance of such supplies and the enormous amount of work and hardship and responsibility that went into the safekeeping and delivery of such. His face grew a little bleak with the memories, for the smashing of his army career was tied up with just such a problem that had gone wrong.

"That's for us, Cloud," said Race Ellison at Steve's elbow. "We'll bring the wagons down and load this afternoon and get everything tucked in and ready for a start tomorrow morning. There's a time element tied up in this freighting contract and the quicker we get on the trail the more to our advantage. Now there are things we got to talk over, and I know you're sick to death of *Spartan* grub, so we'll eat uptown and talk over our business at the same time."

It was a change, but little else, for Calumet was a rough town inhabited by rough men. Steve Cloud and the Ellisons ate in a drab little hash house that was hot and frugal and barren. While he ate, Steve listened to Race Ellison explain the freighting venture.

"There were two bids on the contract to freight in government supplies from here to that new army post, Fort Staley. Ours and that of Grimes Fallon and Hack Overgaard.

66

We got it, and they didn't like their licking a little bit. They've made some pretty strong talk of throwing trouble in our way. I don't know what they think they can do, but they've a reputation for being pretty tough customers, so we'll be smart not to take any unnecessary chance with them."

"I've heard of Fort Staley," said Steve. "That's Jicarilla Apache country. Mean customers, the Jicarilla. Not quite as bad as the Chiricahua, but definitely worse than the Mescalero. But any Apache, when he wants to cut loose, can be poison. You've arranged for military escort?"

Race hesitated slightly. "Not exactly. No need of it for the biggest part of the trip, but the military will be on the lookout for us when we begin to get close to Staley."

"I'd like it better," said Steve gravely, "if we had that escort right from the start. How long do you figure the haul will take?"

"With luck, a couple of weeks, but as a safe average nearer three. Some pretty rough, wild country on the way."

"You've been over the route, of course?"

Race colored as he shook his head. But he said quickly, "A very good friend has, though, and has given me all the data concerning it."

"My friend," said Steve, "you certainly

have got a gambler's heart. You understand, of course, that there must be supply posts along the way? Places where you can feed and water your mules, and where you can pick up replacements, for mules have been known to play out on long hauls, you know."

"That's all arranged for," declared Race. "This same friend of mine has been working on that angle, setting up a series of stations along the route. Not only to take care of our freighting outfits, but in anticipation of a stage route and the influx of settlers sure to come over the same road once the military at Staley have taken care of the Apache threat."

Race went on with growing enthusiasm. "There's a lot of mighty fine country around Fort Staley, I understand. Country for cattle and farming. Calumet here is the nearest supply point. By opening this supply route and making good on this government contract, it means we'll be all set for the days when the settlers start moving in, and supplying them will really be big business. Oh, this is the opportunity of a lifetime all right."

"No doubt," said Steve, a trifle dryly. "But let's remember that as yet the Apache question is far from settled. I'd still like to have that military escort all the way in."

Lynn Ellison had been listening quietly. Now she spoke up. "You make it sound as though we might run across some Apaches as soon as we leave Calumet. Surely you exaggerate."

Steve fixed her with a glance so steady as to cause her to color slightly. "Miss Ellison, no man can put in several years fighting the Apache without learning considerable about them. He either learns these things, and quickly, or he doesn't live. To begin with, the biggest mistake he can make is to try to predict the Apache, for the Apache is quite unpredictable. Besides that he is a merciless and magnificent warrior. And he is smart. Fort Staley is a relatively new post, and the Apache knows that every new post established and maintained is another step toward his own defeat and subjugation. And above all the Apache knows that such a post is utterly dependent upon a steady stream of supplies for its life. So the logical move from his point of view is to try to disrupt and cut off that stream of supplies. And the Apache is always deadly logical about such things."

"Perhaps," said Race Ellison. "But I never heard of anyone who ever saw a hostile Apache within fifty or seventy-five miles of this river."

"Those who might have told you different were probably dead before they knew what hit them," said Steve, in that same dry tone. "Distance means nothing to an Apache. Between dark and dawn he'll cover an amount of country a white man can hardly credit. There is only one safe rule concerning the Apache, believe me. And that is to expect him at any time, in any place, and be prepared to act accordingly. I'm not trying to discourage you or alarm you unduly. I'm merely giving you the facts as I have learned them."

The thump of bootheels sounded at the door, and Steve saw Lynn Ellison start up with pleasure and eagerness. "It's Blake, Race. When he left the *Spartan* at Ehrenberg he said he'd be at Calumet as soon as I was or shortly after."

Both the girl and her brother got to their feet, and Race let out a shout of welcome. "Blake! This is fine! Come here, man, and comfort us. Steve Cloud here has got us all worried about Apaches."

Steve had been sitting with his back to the door. Now he got up and turned, his face going quiet, almost taciturn. It was Blake Ollinger all right, dusty from hard riding, but moving easily and with the same arrogant swagger. His hat was pushed back and

70

his mane of tawny hair lay thick and long against the back of his neck. He was smiling. He made a boldly handsome figure.

Ollinger shook hands with Race Ellison, then turned to the girl. "I've ridden twenty hours straight," he said, "just for the pleasure of looking at you again, Lynn. And of course I'm not disappointed."

It was flamboyant and overdone and it deepened Steve Cloud's dislike and aversion of the man. Lynn Ellison laughed with just a hint of embarrassment. "I'd have been here tomorrow, Blake. I'm pretty substantial."

Ollinger swung his glance to Steve Cloud, his brows lifting questioningly. Race Ellison said, "You've met Steve Cloud, of course, Blake. He's decided to sign on with us. He knows the wild country and he's had experience with the Apache."

"So I've heard," drawled Ollinger mockingly. "He knows when to take 'em and when to leave 'em alone — eh, Cloud?"

Steve, loading up his pipe, said nothing. Race Ellison, sensing the sudden thin strain, spoke up again. "Blake is the man who is setting up that string of supply posts along the trail that I spoke of, Cloud. We more or less figure on working this thing together, he and us."

"That's fine," said Cloud bleakly. "Now, if we're going to load those wagons, we might as well get at the chore. If you want to make that early start tomorrow we want to make sure all the stray details are taken care of. I'll meet you out at the corrals."

Steve turned and went out, tall, lean, quiet striding. This sudden appearance of Blake Ollinger and the word of how he was tied in with this freighting venture were definite jolts. It was inevitable now that his and Ollinger's trails would continue to meet and cross and that the animosity which lay unspoken between them would pile up until, inevitably, there must come an open clash between them. Ollinger would no doubt see to it that he was steadily reminded of the past, and would spread the word and distort the truth which lay behind Steve's departure from his trade as a soldier.

Considering these probabilities, Steve's first enthusiasm for this new venture began to dry up in him and stirrings of doubt arose. Maybe he'd be smart if he told the Ellisons he'd changed his mind. It wasn't too late for that. For the *Spartan* was still tied up at the landing and he could go on upriver with her.

Immediately he thrust this idea aside, for a certain grimness and a realization of stark, cold fact had been growing in him over the past weeks. A man couldn't run away from facts forever. If he did, he was lost, for no man could ever run away from himself. And what a man believed of himself was far more important than what others might believe. He had to make a stand somewhere and lick this thing, once and for all. Here was as good a place as any.

At the wagon camp was Pete Orrick, squatting in the shade of a towering freighter, watching a stocky, powerful, still-faced Mexican at work about the wagon with a monkey wrench and a pail of axle grease. Pete was looking better, and he showed Steve a small grin.

"Now don't you go tryin' to tell me I ought to be layin' up on a bunk somewhere, sweatin' an' frettin' myself to death. I'm doin' fine right here, watchin' Bueno work. With him workin' an' me bossin', we aim to be sure these wagons are all full greased an' ready to roll. The arrangement suits both of us." To which Bueno agreed with a wide and cheerful grin.

Two men came down the short trail from town. One was lank, desert blackened, with a tight, shrewd mouth and pale eyes. The other was burly, with broad, flat features, crude and coarse. They stood for a time at the edge of the meadow, looking things over. Bueno, spotting them first, jerked his black head, and Pete, following the nod, started up, growling.

"Fallon an' Overgaard! Now what would those two slickery whelps be wantin'?"

The two men answered Pete's question by coming over, and the lank one spoke to Steve. "You're Cloud — Steve Cloud?"

Steve eyed them coldly. His nod was curt. "That's right. What do you want?"

"A word with you. I'm Grimes Fallon and this is Hack Overgaard. You got a minute, maybe?"

"Is it necessary?"

"We think so."

Steve was remembering what the Ellisons had told him about these two men. Here was the opposition that had bid against the Ellisons on the freighting contract and lost. What the pair might have on their minds was hard to figure, but there was only one way to find out. Steve led the way off to one side, then swung around to face them.

"Well?"

"We won't waste time beatin' around the bush," said Grimes Fallon. "You're signin' on with the Ellisons?"

"Pretty obvious that I have, isn't it?"

"How much is Race Ellison payin' you?"

74

"That's between Ellison and me."

Fallon shifted his cud of tobacco, spat. "Whatever it is, Hack and me'll double it should you take on with us."

Steve stared at the man, trying to get behind the pale eyes, but without much success. "You don't know me from Adam's off ox, Fallon. Which doesn't make your proposition ring very true."

"We know all about you," said Fallon. "All we need to know, anyhow. Hack an' me can use your likes. And we're always willin' to pay high for what we want."

Steve shook his head. "It still doesn't smell right. Not interested."

"You better be!" This was Hack Overgaard, speaking for the first time, his voice as rough and coarse as his physical appearance.

Steve's eyes went cold, but before he could reply to the threat, Grimes Fallon broke in swiftly. "Hack — you shut up! Let me handle this. What Hack means, Cloud, is that folks generally profit by playin' along with us."

"And they don't — if they don't, is that it?"

"Well," said Fallon slowly, his pale eyes fixed unwinkingly on Steve, "as long as you want to put it that way, why — yes,

75

that's just about it."

"I don't bluff or scare worth a damn," rapped Steve curtly. "You're wasting your breath and my time. And now that we've got that clear, here's something else. You're in the wrong wagon camp. Get out of it!"

Fallon's eyes pinched down. "Oh, one of those proud monkeys, eh? Well, now —"

"Git!" Steve snapped.

Grimes Fallon's laugh was thin and mirthless. "Nothin' so busted an' useless as a busted military man. You, my friend, will find that out. You should have listened more agreeable. Come on, Hack!"

Taking the growling and muttering Overgaard by the arm, Fallon steered him off through the wagons, down across the meadow toward the river and the landing where the *Spartan* rode at rest. Steve watched them go, then went back to where Pete Orrick and the Mexican, Bueno, waited.

"What did those two roosters want?" demanded Pete. "Nothin' good, I bet."

"They offered me a job," explained Steve dryly. "I didn't take it."

Now it was Race and Lynn Ellison and Blake Ollinger who came down across the meadow, and Race waved a beckoning arm. Steve, his face inscrutable, went over, his swift glance marking the expressions of these three. Ollinger had his usual faintly mocking smile, while Lynn Ellison looked sober and Race a little stern.

"I didn't know that you knew Fallon and Overgaard," Race said.

Steve shrugged. "I don't. Never saw 'em before in my life."

"You seemed to be talkin' pretty confidential with them," Blake Ollinger murmured.

So now Steve got it. And the realization held him silent while his glance swung slowly over these three, and in each of them he saw a doubt, a faint suspicion. Into Steve's eyes swept a sudden dark rashness and turbulence. He laughed curtly.

"So that's the way it is, eh? Well then, we better get a few things straight right now, once and for all. I told you I never saw Fallon and Overgaard before. How they knew that I was going to work for you I don't know, Ellison. But they did. And they tried to hire me away from you at double the wages you'd pay me. I turned them down flat. So much for that."

Steve swung his glance to the girl. "My going to work for you and your brother was your original idea, not mine. Twice you asked me to. The second time I agreed.

77

You" — and he looked at Race again — "seemed to be in accord with your sister on the idea. So we made the deal. I'm the same man now that I was then, no better, no worse. Either you still want me or you don't. That's what will have to be settled here and now. You want me or you don't. And if you do, why, then, you trust me. But if you don't trust me, then you don't want me and I don't want the job. Which is it to be — yes or no?"

"It would seem to me," murmured Blake Ollinger, "that —"

Steve cut him short. "You don't figure in this, Ollinger. Nobody asked for your opinion. And just you be patient. I'll get around to you in a minute." Then to Race Ellison, with deepening harshness, Steve said, "Make up your mind! You want me or you don't."

Steve saw answering anger building up in Race Ellison's eyes and he thought that here was the end of a new trail even before it began. But then it was Lynn Ellison, not her brother, who spoke.

"There is no need of this. Mr. Cloud is quite right — and justified. We owe him an apology, Race."

Race hesitated, then burst out gruffly, "Oh, sure. You're right, sis. Cloud, I'm sorry. I'm not doubting you. It's just that I know how much Fallon and Overgaard would like to block our trail and keep us from making good on our contract. Let's forget it!"

Steve nodded. "That's settled, then. But there is something else." He turned and stepped close to Blake Ollinger, and now he was all hard and thrusting challenge. "This seems to be the time and place to clear the air, Ollinger. And this part is just between you and me. You fancy yourself with a gun, it seems. You got one notch for yourself down at Yuma. You got another at Wickenburg. These I know of. There may be others, and probably are. It's a record that might scare some, but it doesn't impress me in the slightest. So now I'm telling you to keep off my heels in the future.

"Frankly, I don't like any part of you, Ollinger. I don't like your sneers or your wisecracks or your strut. I doubt very much you're the pure wolf you make out to be. The really tough men I've known never felt any need to advertise it. So — leave me alone, strictly. Else I'll take your pretty little gun away from you and choke you with it. Now you know!"

Few men had ever dared speak to Blake Ollinger in this fashion. His face first paled then went almost black with fury, his eyes taking on a hard, killing shine. Steve set himself, ready to level a wicked smash at Ollinger's twisted mouth. But Race Ellison stepped between them.

"Stop it! There's no sense to this sort of thing. Lynn, get Blake out of here!"

Lynn Ellison caught Ollinger by the arm, tried to lead him away. He threw her hand off roughly, glaring at Steve. But Lynn caught at him again, talked to him, her voice low and pleading. She was very pale.

Gradually Ollinger quieted. He even won back a hint of his mocking smile, and his voice was only a trifle thick when he said, "There's a lot of time for a lot of things, Cloud. We'll see!" Then he walked away with Lynn Ellison.

Race Ellison, facing Steve, spoke with new anger. "Damn it, Cloud, that's not going to help matters at all. What the devil's the matter with you? Blake's never done you any harm, has he? I told you he's the one who's putting in the way stations along the route to Fort Staley. We're going to have to work closely with him all the way, and we can't stand for a fracas between you and him every time you meet, which will be often enough. I never realized there was this sort of feeling between you and I don't know of any reason why there should be."

Steve shrugged. "Call it one of those things. Two men meet and the sparks fly. Something in their natures just don't jibe. Frankly, I don't like the man and he certainly has little use for me. I suggest you let him know, once and for all, that I'm working for you and your sister, not for him. And I give you my word on this. There'll be no further trouble between Ollinger and me so long as he keeps his mouth off me. Is that fair enough?"

Race, still troubled, nodded slowly. "That's fair. I'll speak to Ollinger. And I don't suppose I have to remind you how much this project means to Lynn and me? If we put it across, we're made. If we don't, we're busted — flat! If I get a little overanxious at times, remember that, will you?"

4

Strings of mules were made up and harnessed, and the wagons, one after the other, rumbled down to the landing, where the great mound of army supplies was loaded. Steve Cloud was very particular about the loading, seeing that the heavier stuff went in first and that everything was compact and snug.

"You never know, in Apache country, when you may have to make a run for a good defense position," he told Race Ellison. "And a wagon packed wrong, so that the load can shift, can upset and raise the devil with your plans. The time to make sure about these things is before you start."

When the loading was done, the wagons were rolled back to the meadow, where water kegs were filled, feed racks on the sides of the wagons stuffed with wild hay, grub boxes packed, and a dozen other odds and ends attended to.

It was dusk by the time all was in readiness for the start early next morning. Pete

Orrick and Bueno and the rest of the wagon men camped right there by the wagons. Steve Cloud spread his blankets under one of the wagons, then went uptown to eat. In the hash house he saw Race and Lynn Ellison at a table with Blake Ollinger.

Ollinger was just about to leave. He stood up as Steve entered, shook hands with Race and the girl, holding the latter's hand for a lingering moment before moving out with a confident swagger, ignoring Steve completely.

Steve, about to take a place at the counter, heard his name called, turned, and saw Race Ellison beckoning to him, so he went over to the table and took a chair.

"Blake is pulling out tonight," said Race. "He'll check things along the trail and send word back to us if he runs across anything that isn't quite regular."

Steve nodded. "Good idea. Always smart to have a scout or two out ahead of a wagon train in Apache country."

"Something else that should interest you," Race said. "Blake applauds our choice of you for wagon boss. He looked over the way you had a couple of the wagons packed and he said you definitely knew your business."

Steve frowned slightly. "That surprises

me. I can hardly imagine Ollinger recommending me for anything but sudden death and a deep grave."

Lynn Ellison spoke up swiftly in Ollinger's defense. "You misjudge Blake. He's vitally interested in seeing Race and me make good with this freighting contract and is willing to put aside all personal feeling to bring it about."

Steve eyed her gravely for a moment, then began his meal. "You people are putting a lot of responsibility in the hands of someone you don't know much about, meaning myself. But if the deal suits you, it suits me. There's one last angle I think I'd better mention. If I'm to be wagon boss, then I must have complete authority over those wagons. Even if, at some particular moment, Race, you and I shouldn't see the setup in the same light. In a trail like we're setting out on, morale is everything. And nothing can tear down the morale of a bunch of men quicker than divided authority. I'll have to make decisions which I'll feel to be to the best interests of the job, and I don't want them questioned."

At this Race hesitated slightly, but not Lynn. "That's absolutely fair. No one should be asked to shoulder responsibilities unless given complete authority to guard them. Neither Race nor I will interfere, Mr. Cloud."

Steve swung his head sharply. "Neither you nor Race! Miss Ellison, you're not trying to say that you expect to go along with the wagon train?"

Startled, she stared at him. "Why, of course I'm going along. I thought you understood that?"

"No," said Steve curtly. "I didn't. And I definitely don't approve. And if I have anything to say about it, you won't go."

Her head went back, her chin tipped up. "But you have nothing to say about it. It's been understood right along between Race and me that I accompany the wagons. You don't think I'd be satisfied to sit around in this miserable little town for weeks and weeks waiting for your return, do you?"

Instead of answering this, Steve turned to Race. "That right? You told her she could go?"

Race squirmed a little. "Yes, I did. And frankly, I see no good reason why she shouldn't. Sis is no languid violet, Steve. She can stand up to hardship as well as any man. And I'd worry more about her if she stayed here alone than having her with us. After all, there's no real danger in it for her. We'll be a strong outfit. No stray Apache is going to bother us too much."

For a long moment Steve was silent, intent on his food. Then he spoke with grave recollection. "I was stationed at Fort Howiston at the time, Colonel Jason Toyen- bee commanding. A member of an emigrant train reached the fort on a foundered horse. He was a brave man, for he had a Chiricahua arrow in his back and was dying as he rode. But he got there and reported the trouble. The Apache had a big wagon train cornered five miles out. We went down there, two troops of us. We had to fight our way in. It didn't do any good. The Chiricahuas had done their work by the time we arrived.

"That was a big train, twice as big as ours will be. We found two people still alive, both men. One died of wounds right after. The other would have been better so. He had lost a wife and two daughters in the affair and was raving. He was still unbalanced when we evacuated him by ambulance to Fort Bowie three weeks later. I saw those three women, after the Apache was done with them." Steve paused, his voice going harsh and taut. "I don't think you people understand the Apache."

Lynn Ellison had gone a little pale, but her eyes held steady. "If that kind of danger does exist, I don't want Race facing it without me. I'm not afraid."

"No," agreed Steve more gently, "I know you're not. But I am. I hope you'll reconsider, both of you. A wagon train in Apache country is no place for a woman."

He had finished eating and pushed his chair back, ready to leave. Now heavy steps sounded at the door of the place. The man who came in and stood just inside the door was hulking and powerful, with thick sloping shoulders and incredibly long arms. A black spade beard, ragged and stained, covered the lower part of his face, and above this, under a low and beetling brow, were eyes that burned with a strangely wild malevolence.

He looked the room over, his glance touching Steve and the Ellisons, then moving on. He seemed to be looking for someone, and, not finding them, turned and plowed heavily out into the night again.

Steve Cloud heard Lynn Ellison catch her breath, while Race Ellison mumbled — "Brokaw! Jess Brokaw! He's on the prowl and that means trouble for somebody!"

"Tough-looking customer, that," drawled Steve Cloud, reaching for his pipe. "Looked like something out of a jungle."

"All of that," said Race. "Last I heard of him he was in Ehrenberg. His usual hangout is one of the lower river ports. Wonder what could have brought him up this far? There's a man who is all pure brute. He's known as 'the bad man of the river,' and a good one to stay away from. There are at least three authentic cases where he has killed men with his bare hands. And those he don't kill he manages to cripple up. I wonder if there's anything to that talk we heard, sis — that he's hired on with Fallon and Overgaard?"

"He'd make a good pair with Overgaard," said Steve, getting to his feet. "From what I saw of Overgaard, they're about the same stripe. But that crowd is the least of my worries. I'm thinking about you in Apache country." He looked at Lynn Ellison. "Won't you reconsider and stay here in Calumet?"

Lynn shook her head. "I'm going along. I can't help but feel you magnify the danger, Steve Cloud."

Steve stood for a moment, brooding. Then he shrugged. "I can't stop you from coming along if you insist. Well, they say there are two ways to learn in this world. One is by listening to sound advice. The other is the hard way, the tough way — which is by experience. It's your choice. I'll see you folks in the morning."

Steve paid his score and went out, a man

big in his own right, yet with a lean and tempered bigness, rangy and full of rawhide toughness, with the long, flat muscles that hold speed and deceptive power. Watching him, Race Ellison murmured, "Perhaps he's right, Lynn. After all, he does know the desert and what it holds. Maybe it would be better if you stayed here in Calumet until we return."

"No!" Lynn was flatly definite in this. "You're going, so I go. There'll be no more argument about that. No doubt Steve Cloud does know the desert and the Apache, but I can't help but feel he's exaggerating things. Even if he wasn't, I'd still go along."

Studying the angle of her chin, Race saw that further talk on the matter was useless.

Outside, the night lay warm and thickly dark, with that peculiar velvet-deep blackness which can precede a late-rising moon. A man, thought Steve Cloud, could sense the presence of the river even though he could not see it. The smell of it for one thing, the odor of dank moistness and the heavy breath of mudbank and sluggish backwater. The bitter, wicked old river!

Well, he'd soon be away from it, back in the dry, harsh magic of the desert which, strangely enough, a man could hate and curse for its never-relenting hostility, hardship, and danger, yet at the same time love for its sheer, almost mystical beauty at sunset, at night under the stars, and in the steel-gray dawn before the sun came up to renew the everlasting conflict.

Out of the blackness a voice came at Steve, a rumbling, hoarse and almost animal growl. "You're Cloud?"

Steve spun to face the words. "That's right. What about it?"

The answer was a man's heavy bulk lunging at him, carrying with it a feral, throaty note of sheer ferocity. Steve had but a split second in which to sense an impression of the shadowy figure, but he knew that he had seen this man standing in the doorway of the hash house but a few moments before.

Jess Brokaw! The bad man of the river!

The next instant Steve Cloud was fighting for his life.

A man with numerous instances of conflict behind him developed a strange sense about such things. He came to know, for instance, when the Apache was merely making a harassing attack which an alert defense and a moment or two of stern action could turn and disperse. He also came to realize an all-out attack that meant a fight to the death — literally.

These things had Steve Cloud met and lived through and grew to know about. And so he knew instantly that here, in this dark street of the tawdry little river town of Calumet, just such a final, ruthless, all-out battle was on his hands with this man-brute, Jess Brokaw. This "bad man of the river," as Race Ellison had named him. This brute out of another age, who killed or crippled men with bare hands.

Sheer instinct told Steve that at all costs he must not let Brokaw come to close grips with him. That would be where Brokaw would excel and be most fearfully dangerous; where he could get hold of a man with those mauling paws and long, ropy, simianlike arms. So Steve whirled aside, dodging low and spinning clear of Brokaw's reaching hands.

Not completely clear. One of Brokaw's clawing paws swept across the flat of Steve's shoulders and, as though the cloth of it was tissue paper, literally wiped the shirt off Steve's back. And those gouging fingers seemed to plow scalding furrows in the flesh underneath.

But Brokaw had missed in his first charge and he came around in his thwarted lunge, cursing heavily. Already half-crouched, Steve came up, lifting and driving with all his weight and power. He did not have a clear target, such as an angle of a jaw to hit at. But he did have the shadowy area of Brokaw's face, and this was what he hit with the hardest punch he'd ever thrown in his life.

He felt the shock of its landing run clear across his back, and it left his right hand and wrist momentarily numb. Even such a burly brute as Jess Brokaw was not impervious to such a savage smash. It stopped him and shook him all over. It did more. It split the flesh to the bone under his left eye and his beard was immediately soggy with streaming blood.

Steve made the most of this immediate advantage. Hardly had that first blow landed than Steve had a left winging, then another flailing right. Both landed and, while not so powerful as that first lethal shot, momentarily bewildered Brokaw and sent him floundering and stumbling.

But the brute was deep and lusty in Jess Brokaw and he shook off the effects of three blows that would have knocked all senses clean out of an ordinary man. The feral growl in his throat lifted to an enraged roar, and he came rushing in for a second time.

A wave of desperation washed through Steve Cloud. He had just landed three of the hardest punches he'd ever thrown in his life, and all the effect they had was merely to stagger Brokaw and befuddle him momentarily. Had Steve a gun, he'd have shot Brokaw dead then and there. But he had no gun, and the bar of a hitch rail was against the small of his back and Brokaw was bearing down on him again. Steve ducked under the rail and sought the wider freedom of the street.

The oncharging Brokaw struck the hitch rail, broke through it like a mad bull through a flimsy corral fence, then bore down on Steve anew.

For the next thirty seconds only one thing saved Steve Cloud. That was speed of foot. The power in Jess Brokaw was a crushing thing, but it was also ponderous. And so, by ducking and weaving and side-stepping, Steve Cloud managed to keep clear. Again and again he smashed rapier blows into Brokaw's face, into his thick, bearish torso. But these blows seemed merely to infuriate Brokaw the more, and now his roars of rage echoed all up and down the street, bringing a rush of men who crowded and pushed about in the dark, trying to get some idea of what was going on. Finally one of them got the answer and yelled it.

"It's Jess Brokaw! He's out to massacre another poor devil!"

Steve Cloud neither saw nor heard any of this. His whole consciousness and world were filled by this lunging, cursing, roaring brute of a man who was seeking to come to close grips with him and so destroy him. And Steve kept on dodging and side-stepping while all the time winging in cutting, blood-bringing punches.

It was like hitting something driven by more than mere human life. And Steve knew he couldn't keep it up much longer. Already his arms and shoulders were growing numb and weary from the tremendous effort he'd put into his blows, with an effect which merely maddened Brokaw the more. Sooner or later Brokaw would get hold of him. And that would be the end.

Twice Brokaw almost got him. Once those clawing paws slid down Steve's left arm, shredding the last of his shirt from him. Another time they clawed across Steve's shoulders again, slipping only because of the sweat and the slime of blood brought by the first clawing. But the third time . . . more!

It came in a wild, sweeping blow, almost spent in force when it struck Steve across the side of the head. Even so it filled his world with blinding lights and picked him clean off his feet and sent him rolling over and over in the dust of the street. He ended up among the fragments of the hitch rail, which Brokaw had smashed through during that berserk charge.

Dimly, Steve Cloud was aware of a woman's broken cry and of the wolfish howl of the crowd anticipating the final brutal finish. And then something snapped in Steve, a sudden loosening of the mad, wild forces of pride and of bleak, bitter courage and of a ferocity to match that loose in Jess Brokaw.

Steve came up out of the wreckage of the hitch rail before Brokaw could get to him. And he came up with a length of heavy timber in his hands. He swung it high and brought it clubbing down. It crashed against Brokaw's head and it stopped him, left him tottering. Again Steve Cloud swung that club, swung it wickedly, brutally. He swung it a third time. It splintered in his hands with this third smash, but it brought Jess Brokaw down in a ponderous, bloody, stricken heap.

If the club had not splintered, Steve would have continued to swing it, for this thing had passed beyond any thought of fair play or sportsmanship. This was stark animal conflict, out of the jungle and of the jungle. Steve threw the broken stump of the club at Brokaw's prone figure then stood over him, feet widespread, body swaying, while the crowd grew utterly quiet, stilled by the savage finish of the thing. The murky light of the lantern which someone had brought flickered across Steve's face and naked shoulders, striking up a turgid shine of sweat and blood.

Steve's chest lifted and fell in shuddering gasps as his breath rasped raw and salty in and out. Abruptly he turned and walked away, stumbling a little as he went.

Behind him he left an awed crowd. Back in the shadows Lynn Ellison clung to her brother's arm, her face dead white, silent tears running down her cheeks. And Race Ellison was muttering over and over — "He beat Brokaw! Steve Cloud smashed Jess Brokaw at his own rough-and-tumble game. There was history made this night along the river!"

Steve Cloud headed for the meadow and the wagon camp. His step gradually steadied, but he moved slowly, deathly weary and drained. It was as though he had poured all the accumulated energy of a lifetime into one short minute of mad, explosive effort. His belly muscles were knotted, while those along his thighs seemed all flabby weakness. His fists felt like lumps of clay, and a deadening ache ran all through his arms and across his shoulders. It seemed he could taste his own blood in his throat. And his head was one big throb from the effects of that single glancing blow Jess Brokaw had landed.

The wild racket in town had carried clear to the meadow and men were stirring and shouting back and forth there. A single small campfire was burning, and Steve headed for this. It was Pete Orrick and Bueno, the Mexican, who pounced on him as he plodded slowly into the firelight.

"Steve!" squalled Pete Orrick. "My God, boy, what you been up to? Who — why — ?"

"Jess Brokaw," mumbled Steve. "He jumped me. I — I clubbed him down like some damn mad animal. Not human — that fellow. Fresh from a jungle —"

Pete and Bueno took over. They spread blankets by the fire, made Steve lie down on them. They explained briefly to the mule skinners who came crowding around, then shooed them back. There was hot water on the fire, and Bueno went to work with this, gently washing down Steve's clawed back and shoulders and cleaning the sweat and blood from his face. Pete produced a bottle of whisky from some place and Steve took a good drag at this. And all the time Pete kept chanting in a sort of dazed delight.

"He beat Jess Brokaw! God's name — the boy beat Jess Brokaw!"

Steve began to get some of it back. When Bueno had finished cleaning up Steve's lacerated back and smeared it with some kind of cooling salve, he sat up and struggled into a fresh shirt that Pete produced. Right after that Race and Lynn Ellison came hurrying up.

"Steve!" cried Race. "You're all right?"

"Good enough," answered Steve, slowly and with some huskiness. He got to his feet, pushed back towsled hair. "Yeah, I'm all right." Then with growing harshness, "Did I kill him? I tried."

"You didn't kill him, but you sure cut him down to size," exclaimed Race. "Man! I don't see how you did it."

"I don't, either," admitted Steve. "Except for that club I managed to get hold of —" He shrugged, leaving the rest to conjecture.

"But what made him jump you? You didn't have any words with him, did you?"

"Nary a word. When I left the eating house there he was, waiting. He called my name, and when I answered he came for me. Maybe it was Fallon's and Overgaard's answer to me for turning them down this afternoon. I intend to find out."

Steve let his glance swing past Race to meet Lynn's eyes where she stood a couple of steps behind her brother. Her face was shadowy and he couldn't get what was in her eyes. "If you saw that," he said, "you saw a dirty, brutal mess. But mild alongside an Apache row."

She did not answer, and Steve turned away. "Me for the blankets. I feel the need of them."

Weary and emotionally drained as he was, Steve still found trouble getting to sleep. He seemed deep drugged with a sort of physical and mental lethargy, his mind muffled with questions that ran in slow and heavy sequence. The different phases of the fight with Jess Brokaw came back to him, and he marveled that he'd come out of the affair a victor. What a ponderous brute Brokaw was! You threw a fist at him with every ounce of power you had in you and it was like throwing pebbles at a bull.

Why had Brokaw jumped him? Neither he nor Brokaw had ever seen each other nor been aware of the other's existence until this night. There was no legitimate cause for the attack except one. Somebody had set Brokaw after him. Fallon and Overgaard?

This was certainly the most obvious conclusion, for Race Ellison had said that Brokaw was a Fallon and Overgaard man.

But was that the only possibility? Steve was remembering the scalding hate he'd seen in Blake Ollinger's eyes earlier this day when he'd told Ollinger off in front of Race and Lynn Ellison. Maybe Ollinger, through money or some other means, had influenced the attack. But this thought led to another strange angle.

Race Ellison had said that Ollinger approved of his selection of Steve as wagon boss. And that hardly added up, either, for as Steve read the man, Blake Ollinger was not the sort to put in a good word for a man he so obviously hated, no matter what the circumstance, unless he had some scheme afoot to discredit or wreak vengeance of some sort. Only one thing was certain, decided Steve somberly. His decision to take on with the Ellisons had tossed him into the middle of a situation which promised anything but a peaceful future.

He stirred restlessly, trying to push aside all this mental turmoil and get the rest his aching muscles cried for. All about spread the wagon camp, still and silent under the stars. The wagons were hooded monsters, ponderous in their waiting. Men slept, while from the corrals came only an occasional stirring. Tomorrow began the big venture, wagons rolling over wild trails, mules toiling and coughing in the dust. There would be the unrelenting sun, the challenge of the miles, and somewhere the lurking, waiting Apache.

This change of thought, from the immediate to the future, brought the relaxation Steve needed. Presently he slept.

The fire which Pete Orrick and Bueno, the Mexican, had built, guttered to graying coals. Pete moved cautiously over for a look at Steve, then went back to collect his own blankets. He spoke softly to Bueno.

"We sleep close enough to the boy to keep an eye on him, Bueno. Awake, he's showed he can take care of himself, but while he sleeps he needs our eyes an' ears."

5

The desert lay all about, ash-gray in the ripening dawn light. Already the wagons were an hour along the trail and the sun not yet up. An early start for the day's travel was vital, for these were the easiest miles — now while the mules were fresh and night's lingering coolness provided a spur to extra effort. Before the sun rose to burn and blaze and sap strength from man and beast. Some things, Steve Cloud had learned by experience, were axiomatic in desert travel — a good start meant a good day's progress.

Steve did not ride a wagon. Instead, he sat a saddle with a good sound horse under him. A Sharps rifle hung in a scabbard under his near stirrup leather and a heavy Colt short gun bulged the holster slung at his belt. Most of the contents of the saddlebags which rode behind the cantle of his saddle was ammunition for these two guns. For this was the desert, and no man could foretell with surety what the future held, except that there would be conflict.

Steve spent the first several miles drifting up and down the flanks of the wagon train, watching the roll of the wagons, the plodding swing of the mules, the adeptness of the skinners and the way they handled their jerk lines and brake straps. For he knew that a wagon train in the desert was like the famous chain which was no stronger than its weakest link.

So many things, minor in themselves at one particular moment, could, at some later date, contribute to a catastrophe. A wagon improperly loaded and balanced. A skinner who punished his equipment and string of mules by clumsy, heavy-handed driving, even a poorly fitting item of harness which could work up a gall on a mule and so lower the animal's strength and worth. These and many other things had his years with the military taught Steve Cloud. For the desert never quit, never let up, and was always ready and waiting to take instant advantage of any man's oversight or carelessness.

Satisfied, finally, that all was as well as could be expected with the wagons, Steve jogged up ahead and joined Race and Lynn Ellison who were riding their horses some hundred yards out ahead of the lead wagon. Lynn was dressed in divided skirt and soft tan blouse and from under the shadow of her hat her auburn hair hung down across her slim shoulders. She gave Steve a quick, inscrutable glance as he dropped in beside her.

A dark bruise lay along one high angle of his jaw, where Jess Brokaw's lone blow had landed. There was a raw stiffness across his back and shoulders, but this was invisible. He had the cavalryman's erect, straight-backed seat in a saddle. Race Ellison said, "Everything's rolling smoothly, Steve."

Steve nodded. "Hope it is a good omen."

"Lynn and I were talking about that affair last night," said Race. "Trying to figure an answer. There's only one. Fallon and Overgaard were out to keep us from having a wagon boss. A particular wagon boss. They must certainly respect your ability in that line. And I still can't figure how you managed to handle Brokaw like you did."

Steve shrugged. "Right now that's history. What concerns me is your sister." He looked at Lynn. "I wish I could persuade you that you shouldn't be here — that you should return to Calumet and wait for us there. The desert is no place for a woman, unless by sheer necessity. And that isn't true in this case."

She tossed her head slightly. "I can ride and shoot — and I'm not afraid. This is my venture as well as Race's. If he can stand it, I can. If there is any real danger, then I intend to share it with him. I thought all that was settled last night. We won't refer to it again, if you please."

She met the sternness of Steve's glance defiantly. "Very well," he said. "If that's the way it must be, that's the way it will be. However, if I'm to be responsible for this wagon train and its safety then you, along with everybody else, must be subject to my orders. Have you any other kind of clothes along except what you are wearing? Jeans and shirt, I mean — man's garb?"

She flushed. "Of course I've no such clothes as that kind. Why should I have?"

"Because, starting tomorrow, that is the kind you must wear. I imagine Pete Orrick can scare up some for you; he's nearer your size than any of us. And you'll wear them. You'll also carry your hair up and hidden under your hat. For what the Apache doesn't know won't help him — or hurt us. When he looks us over, as he most certainly will, the count of what he takes to be an extra man may discourage an attack. On the other hand, the open presence of a woman in our party could very well encourage such an attack."

Race Ellison laughed a trifle skeptically.

"Oh, come now, Steve! Isn't that laying things on a little?"

"No!" rapped Steve curtly. "It's not. Get it out of your heads that I'm talking just to make a noise. I'm not that sort." He swept an arm in a circling movement. "Take a good look at it. The desert. There it is, waiting — always waiting. Its claws are sharp, its fangs long. Never underestimate what it can do to you, for it strikes without warning and with incredible savagery. That's a point I surely hope I won't have to continually argue over with you. It's a big country, and it's swallowed the bones of many a fool."

He lifted his horse to a jog and pulled away up ahead, a thread of bleak anger churning in him. Maybe, of the fools he'd just referred to, he was the bigger one. The bigger one for ever taking on with the Ellisons. Colonel Toyenbee, back at Yuma, had sold Lynn Ellison on the idea that Steve Cloud was exactly the kind of man she and her brother were looking for to take their wagon train safely across the desert to Fort Staley, and he'd been hired on that basis. Hired because he'd had experience with the desert and its ways. Yet when he tried to give thoughtful advice they seemed to view it with a sort of tolerant amusement. Well, by

God — let 'em learn the tough way!

Lynn Ellison stared after Steve's receding back with a certain high-chinned resentment. "It's ridiculous, of course, and I won't do it," she burst out. "Dress in men's clothes, I mean."

"I admit it seems a little farfetched," said Race. "At the same time, Steve could be completely right in this, sis. It might be a good idea to agree with him."

"No! In things that are really important, yes — but in this, no! He's just trying to get even with me for refusing to stay back at Calumet."

Race chuckled. "Now you're being ridiculous. You'd make Steve out as petty and he's anything but that. He's a bigger man than I thought. Don't forget last night. He whipped Jess Brokaw. Jess Brokaw! I still have trouble believing that. But he did it, and I saw him do it. So did you."

The girl was silent a moment. "That still has nothing to do with his trying to tell me what kind of clothes I should wear."

"Yes, it does," insisted Race soberly. "It took more than just physical ability to whip Brokaw. It took mind and heart and a brand of courage not easily come by. A man with that kind of courage in him would never be small enough to be spiteful."

"Perhaps," retorted Lynn. "But I'll still dress as I please."

Steve Cloud made a day of it, scouting out ahead of the wagon train. He rode far, and this was an old story to him and he knew a deep satisfaction at being back at it. The feel of a good horse between his knees, to meet the challenge of the sun and the desert, and to possess the quiet knowledge that he had long since passed its sternest tests successfully — these were good things for a man to know and feel.

The desert, so Colonel Jason Toyenbee had once told him, was an open book to a man smart enough to learn how to read it. To the man who was smart enough to study its signs and portents and learn to understand them, the desert would give up its secrets, and that man need no longer fear it. But to the man who was neither smart nor openminded enough to glean this knowledge, the desert had nothing but contempt and a waiting savagery that would one day dispose of him with brutal and ruthless finality.

Many times had Steve Cloud seen the proof of this plainspoken wisdom. He had done his share of helping bury the awesome reminders. Even guards who, on some lonely bivouac, had let the night's seemingly soft emptiness lure them to an unwary doze and who had paid for this carelessness with an arrow in the back, or a throat cut from ear to ear by an Apache hand they neither saw nor heard. . . .

For the first night the camp was on a flat beside a shallow wash, where lay a couple of sketchy pools of bitter water which satisfied the mules. The humans drew on the water kegs slung to the wagons. Mesquite wood campfires lifted pale against the dark. Steve Cloud, checking all things for the night, was the last to sit up to a fire and food. Pete Orrick handed him his plate of simple fare.

Across the fire Lynn Ellison sat cross-legged, staring into the flames. There was, thought Steve, clear strength and courage in this girl, but there was also a fineness, a certain delicacy which the desert would seize at avidly, should it ever get the chance. Again he found himself wishing she had stayed back at the river, but he realized that it would do no good at all to try to reopen the subject. This girl had a mind and will of her own.

Race Ellison, coming up to the fire, asked, "How do things look up ahead, Steve?"

"Clear enough just now. However, we'll start posting guards."

"Already? Just one day's travel distant from the river? You don't expect Apache prowlers just yet, do you?"

Steve shrugged. "You can never tell about an Apache. So it's wise never to take anything for granted. Besides, we may as well get the men into the habit. A wagon train on a long trail — and the men with it — must shake down into a routine schedule. And the quicker that schedule is established, the quicker it will begin working smoothly. So we start guard duty tonight."

As soon as he finished eating, Steve called all hands together, explained the routine, set up the guard shifts and stationed the first of these. Not half an hour later one of these challenged the approach of a rider coming in from the east. This turned out to be a burly bearded fellow who gave his name as Maslin. He said he'd been sent back by Blake Ollinger to meet the wagons and guide them through to the first of Ollinger's permanent way stations, which they would reach the following night.

There was, declared Maslin, no signs of Apache anywhere along the route he'd just covered, and as this word spread among the wagon men there were grumblings against the prospect of standing a guard shift, especially by one or two who were detailed for the second shift, starting at midnight. Of these, one named Larkin was the most vociferous. Steve Cloud, listening, let them talk, but the gray of his eyes darkened grimly. As the days went on, these fellows would learn who was boss.

Steve had detailed himself to this second and most onerous guard period. He could appreciate that it was a disagreeable chore to climb out of your blankets at a moment of deepest sleep and rest, and then watch the slowest hours of the night creep by to greet the first thin light of dawn. But he was up and moving at midnight hour, checking guard posts, and getting the relief stationed. He himself would take over Pete Orrick's post. But at a final one he found Bueno, the quiet, hard-working Mexican, waiting for a relief that did not show.

To Pete Orrick, Steve said, "Hang on for a few minutes more, Pete. I got to go rout out Bueno's relief."

Bueno's relief was the fellow Larkin, and Steve found Larkin snoring in his blankets. Steve brought him awake with a nudging boot toe. Larkin came up on one elbow, angry and snarling.

"I'm standin' no damn-fool guard duty when there ain't a lick of need for it. You know an' I know there ain't an Apache within a hundred miles of here, Cloud."

Steve reached down, pulled the blankets

off the fellow. "You're hired on to do a job, Larkin," he rapped curtly. "You'll do your full share along with the rest of the men. Get up and moving!"

Larkin hit his feet, ready to fight. But then he remembered that here, facing him, was the man who had whipped Jess Brokaw, the most feared rough-and-tumble fighter along the river. Larkin went surly and defiant.

"This ain't no damn military camp, Cloud. Mebbe you're forgettin' that. I ain't some poor devil in uniform who has to take orders from such as you or go to a guardhouse. You got no right to ask a man to give up half his night's sleep when there ain't no use for it. I can quit this job, you know. An' I damn well will if you keep after me."

"Sure," agreed Steve harshly, "sure you can quit, Larkin. But let's get one thing straight. All you brought to this job were the clothes on your back. Everything else, including a gun, Race Ellison supplies you with. So any time you quit you leave this camp with just what you brought to it — just the clothes on your back, nothing more. No gun, no food, no water. And you walk. If you want to start back afoot for Calumet, you can. It'll be a long, thirsty, hungry jaunt. Make up your mind!"

"Only an Apache would put a man afoot in the desert with nothin' to eat or drink or defend himself with," blustered Larkin, his first belligerence beginning to run out of him fast. "No white man would."

"I would," snapped Steve. "And I will. Either you quit or you don't. And if you don't, you'll do as you're told. Which will it be?"

Larkin cursed again, pulled on his boots, and slouched off to relieve Bueno. Steve went over to Pete Orrick's post and said, "You can hit for your blankets now, Pete."

Pete lingered for a moment. "Most of the skinners in this camp never were back more than twenty miles from the river, Steve. They got no idee what the back desert can be like, I reckon. So, if you have to, use the spurs on 'em, boy."

"I intend to," promised Steve. Then he added gravely, "Not only the skinners have the wrong slant on some things and will have to be corrected, Pete. There are others."

The balance of the night passed without incident and Steve had the camp awake and hustling long before the stars began to fade. And so the wagons were across the wash and rolling ever deeper into the desert before the first faint blush of pink began to wash up in the eastern sky.

There was no way to gloss over the hard monotony of desert travel. Two things were there which no man could change. Time and distance. A mile was a mile, and it took so many turns of a ponderous wagon wheel to cover it, while time was an elemental thing, governed by the lift and fall of the sun. A wise man fought neither of these things that were. He accepted them stoically, built a brand of patience and reserve to match their inexorability.

Tip Larkin was not a wise man. Surly and discomfited from having to stand his shift of guard duty, he was rough with his mules when he harnessed up for the start of the second day's haul, and he was just as bitter and as rough as he drove. As a consequence, by midmorning he had his team frothing and fretting.

At the start Blake Ollinger's man, Maslin, went out well ahead and Steve Cloud went with him. Convinced after several miles of riding that the route Maslin pointed out was the most practical one, Steve left Maslin to go on while he headed back to the wagons, but, true to his old training, quartering the country somewhat as he went. And so it was, when crossing a little area of bare and level sand, he saw something that made him rein in abruptly, stare at the ground for a moment, then lift narrowed eyes for a long and careful survey on all sides. He even reined back and rode two widening circles about the spot, his revolver drawn and ready in his hand. Riding those circles, he overlooked not a clump of mesquite or cactus, nor a small outcrop of scab rock near by.

Satisfied at length that nothing more hostile than several lizards were within the area, he rode back to that patch of sand, got down and studied it very carefully on his hands and knees. Once he lay flat and sighted along the surface of the sand, catching the angle of the sun so that it threw but the thinnest line of shadow along one side of a faint imprint. Finally he went back into the saddle and spurred out to meet the wagons.

He found the whole train drawn to a halt. Something was going on about the third wagon back, which was Tip Larkin's wagon. Race Ellison was there, his eyes angry, his face flushed. Lynn Ellison was there, too, sitting her horse quietly to one side but looking grave and troubled. Skinners from the other wagons had climbed down and were gathered around, saying nothing, but watching and listening with a sort of sardonic truculence. Tip Larkin, perched on the high box of his wagon, was arguing with Race Ellison.

As Steve Cloud rode up, the watching skinners shifted restlessly and a couple of them started edging back toward their own outfits.

"Stay put, everybody!" rapped Steve. "What's going on here?"

Race Ellison whirled on Steve. "It's this fellow Larkin. He's been abusing his mules all morning, Steve. Look at them, all foamed up and fighting wild in their collars. I've warned him twice to lay off nagging the mules and give them a chance. He pays no attention. Now he's threatening to quit. And we can't afford to lay over here while I head back to Calumet to try to round up another skinner to take his place. The damn fool just won't listen to reason and these others seem half-inclined to take his part."

Steve Cloud had been trying from the moment he first met Race Ellison to get a full picture of him. Now he had it. Race was a good man, and honest. He had a shrewd enough business head, but he definitely didn't know the desert and its ways and he didn't know how to handle men too well. In a pinch, Race would fight. But there was a cautious streak in him, a certain bargaining instinct that would cause him to temporize to a certain extent and to waste time trying to find some peaceful solution to a problem where no such solution existed.

Steve said, "Let me handle this, Race."

Steve looked up at Larkin. "Maybe you've forgotten the little talk we had last night, friend. You shouldn't have, for I meant every word of it. Now I'm giving you one last chance to get into line and stay there. Think it over — careful. And before you get too proud, here's something to consider. Out front there about a mile I ran across Apache sign — a moccasin print in a spread of soft sand. So are you going to behave yourself and handle this string of mules as they should be handled, or do you start walking?"

Larkin swung a glance over the hot, still, seemingly utterly empty spread of surrounding country. He laughed defiantly.

"You can't scare me with that Injun talk, Cloud. Ain't even a buzzard around, let alone an Apache. So you get this. I hired on to skin a string of mules, not lose my sleep nights standing some fool guard duty every camp we make, when there ain't a thing to guard against. And the other boys feel just the same as I do."

"That," came Bueno's soft, quiet voice, "is not true, Señor Larkin. You speak for yourself, not for Bueno."

"Or for Pete Orrick, either," cut in Pete.

"You're a plain fool, Larkin. You an' some others in this outfit don't know the back desert at all. You ain't ever been a day's travel away from the river before. But Steve Cloud knows the desert and he knows what's in it. You notice he stood his share of guardin' last night, an' he wouldn't have done that just for the fun of it if it wasn't necessary. You better listen to him."

Tip Larkin spat derisively. "Him an' his highfalutin military idees. I'm remindin' him again that he's dealin' with free men now, not with a flock of poor buggers locked in uniform who don't dare talk back to some pip-squeak ossifer."

"That's your final answer, Larkin?" rapped Steve coldly.

"That's her," leered Larkin.

"All right. You're done. Get down off that wagon and start walking. Bueno will take over your wagon."

"Like hell I'm walkin'," retorted Larkin. "Even with somebody else holdin' this jerk line, I'm still ridin'."

Steve leaned from his saddle, caught the high side of the wagon, swung up on it. Startled, Larkin cursed, swung a clumsy blow which Steve jerked away from. Then Steve's curved arm hooked swiftly; his fist landed with a spat. Larkin tumbled off the lofty

118

wagon box and landed hard and sprawling on the sandy earth below. Steve climbed down after him.

Larkin lurched to his feet, pawed at a bloody mouth, and backed away. He yelled at the other skinners.

"You boys gonna stand for this? You gonna let him kick me around?"

A grizzled, hawk-faced skinner growled, "Yore funeral, Larkin. You started it. Cloud knows what he's doin', an' any of you jiggers who think different stand a better'n even chance of endin' up minus yore hair an' stuck so full of Apache arrows you'll pass as a porkypine. Me, Jake Holcomb, I'm skinnin' my outfit an' doin' what I'm told."

With that, Holcomb went back to his wagon and climbed to the box. The balance, with one or two doing some muttering, followed. Tip Larkin cursed them bitterly, then turned a defiant face on Steve Cloud.

"All right, damn you — I'll walk. But I'm not backtrackin'. I'm headin' on for that first station of Ollinger's. And I'll lay over there until I pick up a chance to ride back to Calumet. To hell with you! I'll be at Ollinger's when you pull in tonight an' I'll give this whole cussed outfit the big laugh about your desert an' your Apache talk. I'll show you who's the fool around here!"

With that Larkin struck out, even mustering a swagger as he passed the lead wagon.

Steve Cloud turned to Bueno. "Think you can do a job of running a jerk line, Bueno?"

Bueno had not been hired on as a skinner, but as a sort of general handyman and roustabout. He had worked around mules a lot but had never handled a jerk line a great deal. But his answer now was to climb up to the wagon box that had been Tip Larkin's seat. As he settled himself and took up the jerk line and the brake strap, he showed Steve a small, white-toothed smile.

"I will do all right, Señor Steve."

Skinners yelled, whips cracked, and mules leaned into their collars. Heavily laden wagons creaked into movement again. Race Ellison, his first anger cooling, turned to Steve with a small show of uncertainty.

"Isn't that being a little extra rough with Larkin, Steve? Putting him afoot, I mean? Oh, I can't blame you for firing him. It was open insubordination on his part. But it wouldn't have hurt to let him ride as far as Ollinger's first station."

"Especially," put in Lynn Ellison, "if, as you said, you really saw some Apache sign."

Steve got out his pipe, packed and lighted it, all the time staring out across the desert.

His eyes were hard, his face grim. "How much," he asked harshly, "does it mean to you people to get these wagons safely through to Fort Staley?"

"Why, everything — of course," answered Race, startled. "I told you it was make or bust with us."

"And you'd let one maverick mule skinner's lazy orneriness jeopardize your whole future?"

"Well, no — of course not. But —"

"Then don't question the way I'm handling this. I know what the desert can do to men, even those who are used to it. It can make them surly, disgruntled, ready to kick over the traces at any excuse. We've got skinners in this outfit who never have really bucked the desert at its worst. If we'd let Larkin get away with his grouch and peeve we'd have had nothing but trouble all the way. Some of the skinners would have rebelled at guard duty, been careless with their mules and outfits, and we never would get through to Fort Staley.

"Get this right, so I don't have to say it over again. Two things hold a wagon train together in the desert, keep it strong and able to fight through. One of these things is discipline, the other is fear of a common danger. The desert and the Apache will

121

supply the last. And while I'm wagon boss I'm going to supply the first — in my own way. That is the way it has got to be." There was flint in Steve's tone as he finished.

"That's all very well," said Lynn Ellison, flaring slightly, a glint in her eyes and her manner stiffening. "But needless brutality doesn't have to be part of that discipline. You sent that man off afoot, without food or water. And under this sun —"

"The walk won't kill him and he'll last out the thirst. It will be a good lesson for him," said Steve with stony evenness. "Now you were asleep when the second guard shift went on last night, so you don't know what happened. Larkin tried to refuse to stand his shift. I told him then what would happen to him if he didn't buckle down and hold up his end. I told him he'd leave this wagon train just the way he came to it, with nothing but the clothes on his back. I wasn't bluffing, and he knew it. So now he's made his choice and he'll have to abide by it."

Lynn tried to hold the sternness of his glance but was unable to. And a flush that was largely anger swept her face. On his part, Steve Cloud wondered what perversity had gotten into this girl. She had changed decidedly from the girl who had come to him on the *Spartan* and with fine, fair honesty had thanked him for saving Pete Orrick's life and had apologized for her original attitude toward him. Now she was hostile again and seemed determinedly bent on letting him know it beyond all doubt.

The only answer Steve could figure was resentment on her part for the way he had thrown the gage in Blake Ollinger's face. That must be the answer and, perhaps, because he'd tried to persuade her not to come along on this journey.

"Discipline," insisted Lynn again, "is one thing. But being unnecessarily harsh is something else. I myself feel that you are really overdrawing this Apache danger. So I can't blame Larkin for feeling the same. All yesterday and so far today I've watched and watched, and I haven't seen a thing move that even remotely resembles a hostile human being."

Steve Cloud took a final drag from his pipe, knocked the dottle out against his saddle horn. "You seldom see an Apache until he's ready to drive a knife or arrow into you," he said dryly. "And then it's too late."

He reined around, touched his horse with his spur, rode after the wagons, up to them and past them. Here the far sweep of the country ahead was a gradual upward slope, deceptive but definite, leading to a low crest some miles ahead. The slope fought the big Merivale wagons and they slowed, with the mules leaning ever deeper into their collars as they sweated out the slow and toilsome pull.

Larkin was already well ahead of the wagons and now, as the big freighters slowed against the climb, drew steadily away. Steve followed the plodding figure with his eyes and bleakness pulled at his lips. He held nothing personal against the man, nor had he any desire to inflict any extreme physical punishment upon him. But this example was necessary. It was exactly as he had told Race and Lynn Ellison. Discipline was all important in a project of this sort. One laggard, one trail lawyer shirking his legitimate duties and allowed to get away with it, could take the spine completely out of the whole organization. So there came times when the whip had to be used, and it had to fall somewhere. . . .

Riding with his sober thoughts, Steve heard a horse coming up behind him at a lope. It was Lynn Ellison, with a freshly filled and still-dripping canteen slung to the horn of her saddle. Her eyes were fixed on Tip Larkin, and Steve saw exactly what she had in mind. He swung his horse over to block her way.

"No!"

He watched the anger run all across her face, saw it flame in her eyes. "Let me by!" she flared. "That man up there has a right to some water. I'm taking it to him."

"No!" growled Steve again. "You're doing nothing of the sort. For two reasons. One is that I won't allow you to spoil the effects of a well-needed lesson. The other is that I saw Apache sign. So you're staying in close to the wagons."

She went a trifle pale as the anger piled up in her. "When my brother and I hired you as wagon boss, that did not convey the authority on you to order me around, Mister Cloud. I'll ride where I please and when I please."

She spun her horse slightly, used her quirt, and dashed past Steve who, swearing in soft and brittle anger, spurred after her. It was a quarter of a mile race before he could catch up with her, lean over, and grab her rein. She half-lifted her quirt, as though she would use it on him.

"Steady!" rapped Steve. "That wouldn't do either of us a bit of good. What the devil's got into you, anyhow? I'm not trying to order you around unnecessarily. Use your head. This is straight common sense I'm trying to put across. If I remember rightly, one of the reasons you gave for wanting me to go to work for you and Race was because you felt I had some knowledge of the desert. Well, if that be true, why insist on going against my advice? If you feel you know more about the desert than I do, and understand the handling of men better, then there's no sense in you paying me wages. I might as well drag out of this game right now."

For a moment she met his glance defiantly, then looked away, biting at her lips. Steve let go of her rein and spoke with lessening harshness.

"If it will make you feel a great deal better, all right — you can take that canteen of water to Larkin. But I'm riding with you."

They went on up the slope at a swinging walk. Ahead, Tip Larkin had disappeared beyond the crest. Underfoot was a stretch of hoof-muffling sand. Then they passed out of this and were over the crest, and of a sudden Lynn Ellison was crying in thin alarm and Steve Cloud was moving as fast as he ever had in his life.

Thirty yards ahead Tip Larkin lay spread-eagled, face down. Standing up rigidly from the center of his back was the feathered end of an arrow. Bent over Larkin's body, scalping knife at work, was a stocky but lithe mahogany figure, naked to the waist, wearing only breech clout and beaded boot moccasins, a sweat-stained brow band holding back lank black hair.

Like an animal, like some fiercely deadly desert cat, the Apache came up and around. Ferociously eager to take Larkin's scalp, the warrior had been so intent on his savage business he had let himself be caught in the open by the sudden and silent approach of Steve Cloud and Lynn Ellison. Now, however, he struck with the speed of a coiled rattler.

Short, sinew-backed bow lifted and twanged almost in one motion. Beyond the flicker of the speeding arrow Steve Cloud saw the dark wildness of the Apache's face, the hard and utter ferocity in the black eyes, the way the mane of black hair was pinched at the temples by that headband of dirty calico. Steve saw something else. He saw that the arrow was headed for Lynn Ellison!

His own move was instinctive, purely. He ripped in the spurs, lifting his horse into a wild, whirling lunge that shot him in front of the girl, and he took the arrow with the broad of his twisting left shoulder while his right hand clawed at his holstered Colt gun.

The shock of the arrow striking was unbelievably heavy. It rocked Steve in his saddle. Just an oversized sliver of wood almost, with a clot of feathers on one end and a chip of desert obsidian on the other. Yet it struck a wicked blow and drove swift and numbing agony deep into the hard muscled round of Steve's upper left arm and shoulder.

Even as the first arrow left the bow, the Apache whisked another from the quiver and was nocking it as he darted like a startled wolf for the shelter of a mesquite thicket short yards away.

Along the barrel of his revolver Steve glimpsed the twisting, darting figure, the half-turned, savagely hating face. Then the heavy Colt blared, leaped, and pounded back in hard recoil. The big bullet smashed home, throwing the Apache sideways, hammering him down, where he writhed a moment, tried to lift up, then collapsed fully, and flattened limply against the earth.

6

It had all been very swift, very explosive. There has been a deadly break in the desert's hot, gray silence and emptiness. Now two men lay dead. Death had struck, leered, passed on.

Harsh as raw metal, Steve Cloud's voice struck at the girl, who sat her saddle like one stunned. "Get back to the wagons — quick! Don't argue. There may be more Apaches around. Back to the wagons, I say, and tell them to be ready for anything!"

She obeyed automatically, too shocked and shaken to think. She spun her horse and raced back over the crest. Colt gun poised high and ready to chop down at the slightest move or sound, Steve Cloud ran cold eyes back and forth over every brush clump, every spot of possible concealment he could see. But there was no further move or sound.

He kneed his fretting, nervous horse close enough to the huddled Apache to see that there was no atom of life left in the crum-

129

pled figure; that big, battering slug had been lethal. Nor was Tip Larkin any less dead, for the arrow, driven at short range, had dug deep.

Pain beat savagely in Steve's left shoulder and arm. He looked at the arrow jutting from his upper arm. It gave him a queer and grisly turn. That arrow, it was stuck deep into his own flesh. He touched it, and the sweat that rolled down his face seemed cold. He set his jaw, lifted his eyes to the bland, still mockery of the desert again. He holstered his revolver, picked up the reins with his right hand, and swung his horse away, riding a wide circle about this deadly crest, scouting for sign.

Steve heard someone yell and looked over to see Race Ellison spurring toward him. As Race came up, Steve's voice rang harsh at him.

"Get back to the wagons! Stay there until I've satisfied myself that there are no more Apaches around. You hear me? Get back!"

"But you, man!" cried Race. "How about you? You got an arrow in you. Lynn told me!"

"I'm doing all right," cut in Steve. "The arrow can wait. Get out of here!"

Steve went on, riding his scouting circle to

a finish before heading back to the wagons. Some of the tension had run out of him now, for he was satisfied that the Apache had been a single, wandering scout who had been unable to hold back the ferocious urge to gather himself a scalp, but had paid with his own life in the attempt.

The wagons stood heavy and still against the slope. A little to one side Pete Orrick had a small fire going, while Bueno was honing a long, slim-bladed knife to razor keenness.

"What's that fire for?" rapped Steve. "We're not camping here."

Pete Orrick faced Steve with grave eyes. "The girl said you had an arrow in you, boy. I see she was right. And it's got to come out. It comes out before these wagons roll another damn foot. In other things you're the boss around here. But in this, me and Bueno, we're tellin' you what we're goin' to do an' we're goin' to make you like it. Git off that horse, boy!"

The brittleness about Steve's lips broke and softened slightly. He gripped his saddle horn with his right hand and swung down. The slight jar of his bootheels, biting into the sandy earth, sent a new wave of hot fire through his shoulder. The sweat started and ran down his face again.

Bueno, observing closely, said, "You see, Señor Steve?"

They spread a blanket in the shade of a wagon and made him sit there. Race and Lynn Ellison came over. The girl's face was white. "I — I wish to help," she said simply.

Pete Orrick shook his head, no sympathy for her in his face. "This may get a mite rough. Leave it to Bueno an' me. Steve's our boy an' we'll look after him." Pete tucked more wood on the fire around a pan of water that was beginning to simmer.

Steve looked at Race Ellison. "Send some men up ahead with picks and shovels. They'll be safe enough. I'm satisfied the Apache was a lone scout, but we got to take care of Larkin and the Indian before we move on. I suggest you send the doubters among the skinners to handle the chore. At least they'll get an idea what a hostile Apache looks like, and maybe the lesson will take."

Bueno's hands were deft and gentle as he slit the sleeve of Steve's shirt and stripped the cloth away from the wound. Examination was swift.

"We have some luck, Señor Steve. The arrow hit the bone, slid off, and came almost through. So we will cut the feathers off, then a little cut in the arm, here — and we push the arrow through cleanly."

"Whatever you say, Bueno," gritted Steve, stung with fresh agony when Bueno touched the arrow ever so lightly.

"Water's ready, Bueno," called Pete Orrick.

Bueno went over, held the blade of his knife in the boiling water to sterilize it, then came back to Steve.

"I will be as swift and easy as I can, señor."

"I know that, Bueno. Fly to it!"

The sky reeled, grew dark, then light, then dark again. The silent world took up a wild, soundless roaring. Sweat drenched Steve from head to foot, slimed his face, stung his eyes. He did not know that Lynn Ellison was watching him, her eyes big and stricken, while she bit her lip and clenched her hands helplessly. He couldn't see that far. For his whole world had pinched down to a tiny focus of light and dark and he couldn't be sure which was going to win over completely, the light or the dark.

And then the savage, slugging agony was gone and only a wicked, smarting ache was left, and the dark went away and the light came back. And Bueno was speaking, in his soft, liquid way.

"It is done, Señor Steve. Now the water, please!"

There was pain when the water touched, but it was almost a pleasant pain after that which had gone before, and after that came a vast and soothing and cooling relief as Bueno smeared the wound with some heavy, dark, pungent oil. Then the bandages, snug and comforting.

Pete Orrick held a canteen to Steve's lips and he drank thirstily. After which he grinned crookedly. "As mule skinners, Pete, you and Bueno are a pretty fair pair of doctors. Now, if I could have a smoke — ?"

Bueno spun up a brown-paper cigarette, put it in Steve's lips, and held a match. Steve inhaled deeply, got to his feet. "Miles to cover," he said tersely. "Let's get 'em rolling!"

The burial party came back to the wagons. They were silent and subdued, but there was surliness in some of them, and several antagonistic glances came Steve Cloud's way. He felt these, but ignored them. He knew what the thought was behind those looks. They were blaming him for Tip Larkin's death. They were thinking that if he hadn't put Larkin afoot, the man would be alive this moment.

Well, that was true enough. That lone Apache, even if he had watched the wagons pass from some hiding place but a few yards

134

off the road, would have made no hostile move against such odds. But what was done was done, and again the desert had demonstrated its oldest truism. Which was that no man could guess what it held in store for him and that there was no mercy in it when it decided to strike. Tip Larkin wasn't the first to die in it, nor would he be the last.

The wagons rolled out the balance of the day without incident. The sun went down into a fiery bed of awesome crimson and a soft, powder-blue dusk was running across the world before the wagons drew to a halt beside a rude ramada and some sketchy corrals where the desert had relented enough to let a seep of water through and a small smear of tough grass stained the center of a little basin.

Blake Ollinger was there to give Lynn Ellison a hand from her saddle with swaggering eagerness. But the girl pulled quickly away from him and came over to where Steve Cloud had dismounted stiffly. It had been a long, tough afternoon for Steve, and he knew a seedy feverishness and draining weakness as he stepped to earth.

"I can't seem to avoid playing the fool," said Lynn quietly. "That arrow was headed for me and you took it deliberately. I — I'm sorry I was so unreasonable. And — thank you."

"Maybe we were both wrong," Steve told her. "Larkin was a troublemaker, but he didn't deserve to die that way. I'm responsible for that and I don't feel a bit good about it."

"There was a difference. You did what you thought was necessary and right. While I knew all the time I was wrong, but I was just too perverse to be sensible. Your shoulder — ?"

"I know it's there," admitted Steve. "But it'll come along."

She went away then, and Pete Orrick came to take Steve's horse. "I can take care of my mules an' this bronc, too, boy," said Pete. "You take it easy. For I'm one feller who figures that we got to keep you healthy, or these wagons will never get through. I've put your blankets down yonder. You go use 'em."

Steve went and stretched out. Campfires winked in the quick dark and cooking odors wafted. Steve, after a short rest, went over to the fire where Bueno hovered and ate his supper there with the Mexican and Pete Orrick. Blake Ollinger had the Ellisons with him at the ramada.

A man came up through the dark to where Steve and Pete and Bueno sat. It was Maslin, Ollinger's scout. He spoke gruffly.

"When you finish eatin', Cloud — Race Ellison wants to see you over at the ramada."

"The hell he does!" rapped Pete Orrick. "Well, Ellison is a whole an' healthy man jest now an' Steve ain't. You tell Ellison if he wants to see Steve, he can find him right here."

Maslin shrugged. "I'm just reportin' what I was told. Fight it out yourselves." He turned and went off into the night. Pete jabbed an angry boot toe at a stray coal from the fire.

"Sometimes I get half mad at Race Ellison. In some ways he's a good feller, but he's so almighty damned concerned with his own affairs he don't always think very far."

Steve got to his feet. "No need making a complete baby out of me, Pete. Do me good to move around."

A couple of candles stuck in empty bottle tops threw a fitful light across the ramada. The Ellisons and Blake Ollinger were seated at a small rough table. There was an extra bench, and Steve sat down there.

"What's on your mind, Race?"

Race Ellison's voice was troubled. "Got a problem on my hands, Steve. A tough one."

Steve shrugged. "The desert's full of problems. Let's have it."

137

"Well, four of my skinners have just served notice." Race paused, not looking at Steve. He seemed reluctant to go on.

"What four — and what kind of notice?" asked Steve, a thread of bleakness creeping into his tone. For he felt that he already knew most of the answer.

"Hart, Jenkins, Plank, and Bascomb — that's the four," said Race slowly. "And they refuse to go any farther than this station, unless —"

"Unless you get another wagon boss, is that it?" cut in Steve.

"That's it. They hold you responsible for Tip Larkin's death."

Steve let his glance run around the table. It came back to Race. "Do you?"

Race was silent, stirring uneasily, frowning down at the table top. Steve laughed shortly, without mirth. "Hell, man! If you got an opinion, speak it. In a way they're right. I was responsible for Larkin's death. But I handled Larkin as I thought best and for the good of everybody. After all, I did give Larkin a choice and I did warn him that I'd seen Apache sign. But at the time several people chose not to believe me. Well, it's your decision to make. You want me or you don't. Which is it?"

Again Race gave that restless squirming

and seemed to find trouble framing an answer. And in this Steve had his answer. A remoteness came over him, a sort of harsh weariness. Race cleared his throat.

"I got to get my wagons to Fort Staley. And I can't get 'em there without skinners. Damn it all, I wish there was some middle ground in this thing."

There, thought Steve, was proof of his earlier conviction. There was Race Ellison for you. A middle-of-the-trail man. Meaning well, a square man to the limit of his lights, but — !

"When it's yes or no there is no middle ground, Race," said Steve. "It's all right with me. I'm probably not near as good as you thought I'd be. After all, they're your wagons and it's your contract. Good luck! And now, a final deal between us. I'm buying the horse I'm riding as well as the guns and other gear you laid out for me. I'd say two hundred dollars would be a fair price."

Steve slid his sound hand inside his shirt and began tugging at the buckle of a money belt.

Race jerked his head around. "Hell with that! I don't want you to cut clear away from me. Why, you saved Lynn's life this afternoon. I owe you plenty for that. And I want you to stay on with us as a scout, working out the route ahead of us. Forget the talk of cutting loose entirely."

Steve shook his head. "I hired on as wagon boss. If I'm not that, then I'm not anything. Besides, if I did scout up some more Apache sign your stout skinners wouldn't believe me. And I never was one to waste my time doing no good."

He counted out the two hundred dollars, pushed it across the table. "That makes us square. You don't owe me anything. I don't owe you anything." He dropped a couple more dollars in front of Blake Ollinger. "For a night's lodging for my horse and myself at this station, Ollinger. That pays everybody."

He got up and went out, a big man, straight-backed with a steely pride. Lynn Ellison's eyes followed him.

"I feel as though you'd hit him with a whip, Race. I don't think you handled that very well. And after what he did for me today —" She paused, living again those stark moments of savage violence, seeing Steve Cloud whirl his horse so that he might take the arrow aimed for her. "No," she said again. "We're not being very fair."

"What else was there left for me to do?" complained Race. "We got to get those supplies through to Fort Staley. And we can't roll without skinners. Believe me, I didn't enjoy this. But when there are two evils a man can only take the lesser one. After all, I can appoint another wagon boss —"

"That's fixed already, Race," said Blake Ollinger. "I'll let you have Maslin in Cloud's place. Maslin's a good man and he'll use better judgment in handling your men than Cloud did. I was wrong about Cloud. I thought he could do the job for you. No question that he knows the desert and the way of the Apache. But he's got that military training in his blood and he's been used to handling troopers. Civilians don't take easily to the military angle. I figured Cloud would be smart enough to realize that."

"Yet he was so right in every way," murmured Lynn Ellison. "He warned us — he tried to tell us. And we wouldn't believe. If he had let me ride on alone after Larkin — !" She shivered, seeing again the sprawled figure of Tip Larkin with that arrow sticking up between his shoulders. And the Apache, lithe and swift and deadly — striking like some cornered animal. Why, if she had been alone — !

She got up abruptly and went out into the night. Race Ellison swore softly. "Lynn's right, Blake. I've given Steve Cloud poor return for what he's done for us."

Ollinger shrugged. "What the hell! He bumps into an Apache that's trying to throw an arrow into his guts. So he shoots the Apache. Any man would have done as much. You can't make Cloud out a hero for that. So stow the regrets — you shouldn't have any. Now I'll go locate Maslin and send him in here to talk things over with you and get squared away for tomorrow."

Ollinger hid the wicked lights burning in his eyes until he was out where the darkness hid him fully. He also had planned things, and they weren't working so well as he'd figured they would. That damned Apache incident had messed things up. He hadn't missed the way Lynn Ellison had pulled away from him and gone right over to Steve Cloud when the wagon train first rolled in that evening. And he didn't like that big, dark light which stirred in the girl's eyes whenever Cloud's name was mentioned.

He had been afraid of Lynn's possible interest in Cloud right from the first. But when, at Calumet, the Ellisons had told him of hiring on Cloud as wagon boss, there was nothing he could do about it but approve the selection. For that trip out to Fort Staley was a long and perilous one and there would be plenty of chance along the way to bring about something that would discredit Cloud in the girl's eyes; Ollinger had several schemes up his sleeve for this.

But now, all because of a damn, prowling Apache, the breakup had come, but not to Steve Cloud's discredit. To the contrary, it was plain that Lynn Ellison felt very guilty and, feeling so, she was going to think more of Steve Cloud instead of less. So there had to be some other out.

Well, Ollinger had one. It was the final one he had figured for Cloud, one that he hadn't intended using until later. All along, Ollinger had promised himself, he'd intended to make sure that Steve Cloud would never get out of the desert alive — never! For a hundred times since it had happened, Blake Ollinger had recalled the way Steve Cloud had told him off, back at Calumet. Recalling it again now, Ollinger's eyes glinted red and his lips thinned back in a soundless snarl. For he had never taken that kind of talk from any man before and then forgotten it. And he never would!

Steve Cloud went quietly back to Pete's and Bueno's fire and dropped on his heels beside its fading coals. The faint reflected glow brought out the lined harshness of his face. Bueno spoke softly.

"Things are not well, Señor Steve. You must rest that wounded shoulder."

Pete Orrick stared anxiously at Steve's face. "What is it, boy? What did Race Ellison want?"

"A little question of who was most important in his plans," answered Steve slowly. "Me as wagon boss — or four skinners who refused to go any farther if I was. Race figured he needed the skinners most — and maybe he's right."

"You mean — he let you go?"

Steve nodded. "As wagon boss — yes. He wanted me to stay on as a scout. But I figured that move was just a little salve to his conscience and I didn't want any of it. So — I'm through."

Pete swore bitterly. "Then that makes two of us."

"Wrong, *amigo*," murmured Bueno. "Three of us."

"No," said Steve, "that won't do. Ellison needs you two to handle a pair of his wagons. He's not entirely to blame in this thing. He's a decent fellow. His biggest fault is that very strain of decency in him that won't let him get as tough with these skinners of his as he ought to."

"What four skinners are bucking over the traces?" demanded Pete. "Bet I can name a couple. Plank an' Jenkins."

"That's right. The other two are Bascomb and Hart."

"Why don't he get real rough with them? Knock their damn ears back."

Steve smiled gravely. "Race Ellison just doesn't understand the desert — and the ways of the men who travel it. Now that they've won one argument with him, they'll figure out something else to kick about. Race is due to find out that letting a bunch of sore heads boss his wagon train isn't going to make it run any more smoothly. That's why you two got to stick around to help him all you can."

Pete was stubborn. "I told 'em back at Calumet that if they wanted me along on this trip then they had to get you to go too. Which meant that if they didn't let you finish the trip, then I wouldn't be there at the finish, either."

Steve looked at dried-up, tempery little Pete and the grimness about his eyes softened. "You're staying on because I want you to, Pete. Not so much for Race's sake, as for that of his sister. If Lynn Ellison wasn't along, then I'd be inclined to wash my hands of the whole business. But it's bad Apache country ahead, and she's going to need some looking after. That's where you and

Bueno come in. And me, while I won't be working for the Ellisons, I'll be around. I'll be out ahead, studying the country. If the trail looks safe and open, I'll stay out ahead. But if I run across any real important Apache sign, then I'll get in touch with you. Now I'm going to get some sleep."

At Steve's request Pete got Steve's blankets, carried them farther away from the wagons and spread them near the corrals. Bueno appeared with some sort of black and bitter draught which he insisted Steve drink.

"There is fever in you, señor. This will drive it out."

Things quieted down. Steve lay back in his blankets, watching the stars, the fever making him restless and keeping him from getting to sleep. The steady throb in his arm and shoulder added to his discomfort, and he knew the impatience of a healthy man against this physical distress. Once soft steps and soft voices passed not far from him, and against the stars he caught the silhouette of the heads and shoulders of two people strolling together. He recognized Lynn Ellison and Blake Ollinger.

A wave of black bitterness rolled over him and a certain determination which had formed in his mind during his talk with Pete and Bueno momentarily weakened. Why, he asked fiercely, give a damn for people who apparently didn't give a damn for him? He'd let one woman make a fool of him and indirectly blast his military career. Why chance another like deal? Better to cut completely loose, ride far, and to hell with it.

Pete Orrick, prowling through the dark, broke in on Steve's dark thoughts. "Wondered if you were still awake, boy. Thought you might like to know that Maslin is the new wagon boss. I'm rememberin' that when Maslin first met up with us back along the trail he reported no Apache sign in the country. But you found some an' you found an Apache. I'm thinkin' we'll be damned lucky to get to Fort Staley all in one piece with that feller bossin' the train."

"Is he placing any guards out, Pete?"

"Nary guard. Says this station is too strong for the Apache to attack. Me an' Bueno don't believe that. So, while we ain't sayin' nothin', we're standin' shift an' shift. Bueno's takin' the second watch, me the first."

"That's smart. Anything else on your mind?"

"Yeah. Miss Lynn. She come by with Ollinger a little while ago. She wanted to know where you were an' how you were

147

feelin'. I told her Bueno an' me had dosed you up with fever medicine an' put your blankets where you'd be quiet. She seemed plenty relieved. Blake Ollinger, he made out like he was pleased too. But Bueno, he says Ollinger's got poison in his eyes, that he's a bad one — *uno malo hombre*. An' I think the same."

Steve was suddenly drowsy. The medicine Bueno had given him was now beginning to take effect. And the news that when she was walking with Ollinger, Lynn Ellison was really trying to find him, concerned over his welfare, in some strange way seemed to ease the grating harshness and restlessness in him. Abruptly he was relaxed and sleep stole over him.

It was black, deep dark when Steve awakened. The world lay very still. By the feel of the air it was some time past midnight. Steve lay without moving, wondering what it was that had jerked him to wakefulness. Some instinct, perhaps, the heritage of his desert years? He propped himself up on his right elbow, looked around. There was a slight and restless stirring among the mules in the corrals. There was uneasiness in the gusty snort of one of them. Steve pushed himself higher, his senses sharpening. And then he reached out for the gun he had placed beside his saddle pillow.

A crouched figure seemed to rise right out of the black earth beside him and all the night was shrieking with a soundless threat. A shout of alarm was forming in Steve's throat and he was clawing desperately for his gun when a solid, crunching thud sounded and the threatening figure shrunk limply and pitched forward, landing across Steve's blanketed legs.

Then it was Bueno's liquid voice, murmuring soft warning. "Quiet, Señor Steve! Give no alarm. There is something here which we must ask only ourselves about. Softly, señor!"

Steve pulled his legs free, crawled out of his blankets. "Bueno! What — who — ?"

"I do not know, señor. But it is not good. A blanket, señor — to shroud a light."

Bueno held the blanket while Steve scratched a match. The faint flicker of light bloomed, held for a moment, then snuffed out. But Steve and Bueno had seen enough.

This was a white man, and he was quite dead, the back of his head pulpy where the steel-shod butt of Bueno's heavy Sharps rifle had landed. But the deadly purpose the fellow had been intent on was proved by the naked knife still clutched in the man's right hand.

"What about it, Bueno?" asked Steve grimly. "Who is he?"

Bueno told his story softly, quickly. He had been on guard about an hour after Pete Orrick had awakened him for his half of the night's guard shift. He had heard that stirring among the mules, that uneasy restlessness, and he had moved softly over to investigate. And he had glimpsed a crouched figure stealing along beside the corral's dark outline.

"He was moving toward where you slept, Señor Steve, and though the stars are far away at this hour I caught one gleam of bared steel. So I came up quickly as he leaned over you and struck with my gun butt."

"You struck hard but well, Bueno," Steve growled. Then he asked again, "Who is he?"

"One of Ollinger's men, señor. I saw him about the corrals with the others when we pulled in. I heard him called Owens. Strike another match, señor."

When Steve did so, Bueno took the knife from the dead man's fingers, then balanced it across his brown palm. Steve exclaimed softly. "That's an Apache knife, Bueno! Chiricahua. I've seen plenty like it on dead warriors after a skirmish, when we came in too fast on them and they couldn't carry away their dead. Yeah — an Apache knife."

"*Si,* Señor Steve. So now I think we understand this thing, you and I. Have I not said that Ollinger was *uno malo hombre* — a bad man?"

"I'd have been found dead in my blankets, an Apache knife in me," muttered Steve. "I'd have been out of the picture and the blame on the Apache. Yet a crude deal — very crude. A smart man who understood such things would ask questions — as to why an Apache would throw away a good knife just to advertise he'd been around? But none here would be smart or shrewd enough to ask Ollinger those things. Bueno, I owe you plenty for this. What will we do with him?"

"You will leave that to me, señor. This will make the devil laugh."

Stocky, powerful Bueno picked up the dead man, prowled noiselessly away. In a little while he was back, grim humor in his voice.

"He will be found when the dawn light comes, señor — out in front of the ramada. It will be amusing to see Ollinger's face when the discovery is made, no?"

"Amusing and perhaps enlightening," Steve murmured. "Bueno, you are a very good friend. I'll be forever in your debt."

Bueno shrugged. "I am just a poor Mexican muleteer, señor. But I like to feel that I am not a whole fool. I know when a man's heart is good and when it is evil. And the one I like and the other I hate. Now get your sleep, señor. Bueno will be watching."

Back in his blankets, with the world still and sleeping once more, Steve Cloud knew that now indeed had his destiny committed him to certain things. This trail to Fort Staley would have to be his trail, even though he would now travel it as his own man. For somewhere, sometime along that trail there must come a final settlement with Blake Ollinger. That much was written. It was in the stars. And now, thinking about it, Steve realized it had been so from the very moment he and Ollinger first met.

Steve realized the truth of something else. Deep down, hidden by his swagger and sneering arrogance, there was a streak in Blake Ollinger. The man was a killer, knowing a certain confidence in his use of a gun. But thinking back to the death of Jeff Turnbell at Wickenburg and of the river tough at Fort Yuma, Steve could see where Ollinger had in each case held the edge and had seized it with explosive ruthlessness.

But that edge would not be there when he faced a man who had seen him for exactly what he was, and would therefore not be caught on the wrong side of that edge. And so, in such case, Ollinger was not eager for an open showdown. Instead, he would strike as he had attempted to this night. From now on, Steve realized, he must never forget that fact. . . .

Before he fell asleep again Steve realized something else. Which was that he felt immeasurably better physically. His head was cool and no longer did he ache in every fiber. His fever was gone, driven out as Bueno had promised it would be, by that black and bitter potion the faithful Mexican had made him drink. Even the torment of his wound had largely left. His shoulder and arm were sore and stiff, but that nagging throbbing was gone.

He curled deep into the warm comfort of his blankets and slept soundly.

7

A man's harsh, startled yell brought the camp awake. Dawn was breaking clear and sharp across the world. In the far eastern distance the ragged crest of mountains was limned against the brightening sky. There was confusion over at Blake Ollinger's ramada.

The word spread rapidly and skinners, mumbling and wondering, hurried that way. Pete Orrick and Bueno came over to Steve Cloud's blankets and Pete helped Steve pull on his boots. Bueno had evidently given Pete the news of the night, for there was a sardonic glint in Pete's eye.

"Now I wonder what all the excitement is about?" twanged Pete. "Mebbe we ought to go have a look, Steve."

"As long as everybody else is, why not?" Steve nodded.

So they went over and joined the group. Race Ellison was there. "Damnedest thing," he explained to Steve. "One of Ollinger's men — fellow named Owens, I believe — was found lying out in front of the ramada,

154

the back of his head knocked in. Nobody seems to have any answers."

"That," said Steve dryly, "is the desert for you. Plenty of things show up in it that don't have any answers."

Blake Ollinger had just given orders to some of his men to carry the dead man away. Now he came over to Steve and Race Ellison. His eyes held a shadowed, uncertain murkiness. "Can't figure it, Race," he said with some heaviness. "Far as I know, Owens was on good terms with the rest of my men. But somebody in your outfit might have had it in for him."

Race turned to Steve again. "Would any of our crowd — ?"

Steve cut him short with a wave of his hand. "Not ours, Race — yours. As of last evening I'm responsible for nobody but myself. Remember? What have your guards got to say?"

Race colored. "Why — ah — Maslin said it wasn't necessary to post any guards. He felt there was no danger here."

Steve, his tone still dry, said, "If that dead man could talk I wonder what he'd say to that?"

Steve was looking straight at Ollinger as he spoke, a faintly cold gleam in his eye. Ollinger looked away.

The group was scattering, and Jake Holcomb, the grizzled, hawk-faced old skinner, was growling. "Late start today — too late. Not even breakfast yet. We better move an' catch up. A late start means long miles, short travel. Early mornin' is the time to cover distance in the desert. Maslin ought to know that. Steve Cloud knew it."

"Damn right Steve knew it," chimed in Pete Orrick. "Steve knew somethin' else too — about postin' guards. But when I asked Maslin about that, he said no guards here. So we got a dead man on one hand an' a late start on the other. There's a lot more to bein' a good wagon boss than a line of smooth talk."

Breakfast was hurried and sketchy. Maslin stumped around, surly and profane. The atmosphere of the wagon camp was edgy and men snapped and snarled at each other. Lynn Ellison, who always slept in one of the wagons, had climbed down and joined her brother at the fire. She took a cup of coffee from him, sipped it, then said, "We've made a mistake, Race — a serious one. I think we ought to try to rectify it right now."

Race knew what she meant, and he answered with some sharpness. "The issue hasn't changed over night. Those four skinners haven't changed their minds. And I still have to have them. Once we get rolling again things will adjust themselves. In all fairness to Maslin, that man hasn't had a chance to show what he can do. We got to give him that chance."

"He knew last night that he was to be wagon boss," said Lynn quietly. "His responsibility started then. So did his chance to show what he could do. I don't see him doing anything to inspire confidence."

Race, harassed by an uneasiness he couldn't deny, grew angry. "Not too many hours ago you were at loggerheads with Steve Cloud yourself. You weren't liking the way he was doing things — not a bit. Why try and blame me?"

"I'm not blaming you, Race. I'm blaming both of us. Only, I'm willing to admit I was wrong."

Steve Cloud ate breakfast with Pete Orrick and Bueno, after which Bueno brought Steve's horse from the corrals, saddled it for him, and helped him pack his gear. Bueno's brown face was bland.

"There are many questions in Ollinger, Señor Steve. But he cannot ask them or he would betray himself. Ay! The devil laughs."

Pete Orrick, coming over, said, "Boy, don't you get too far away from us. If Maslin is a wagon boss, I'm a cockeyed Chinaman. Me, I don't see nothin' ahead of this wagon train but misery. I thought Race Ellison had some gumption. He ain't. He's too soft for the desert. Wish I knew what to do about it."

Race and Lynn Ellison came over to the corrals after their horses. Race looked flushed and angry, while Lynn was sober and grave of eye. Which Steve Cloud noticed, along with the fact that she was no longer in divided skirt and blouse. Instead, she had on jeans and a hickory shirt, both somewhat large for her, and in them she looked like a slim youth. Her hair was done up and hidden under her wide, flat-brimmed felt sombrero. She colored faintly at Steve's glance.

"I'm a little late taking your advice — but I'm taking it. Pete Orrick managed to scare up these duds for me. Do I look as awkward as I feel?"

They were a little apart from the others, with Pete and Bueno busy with their mules and Race getting out the horses. Steve said, "The outfit is very becoming. With some women clothes dress them up. But with a very few it is the woman who dresses up the clothes. You are one of the few."

It was the first really personal note that

had ever passed between them. Lynn's color deepened. "I think you're merely being kind. Your shoulder — how is it?"

Steve smiled down at her. "Surprisingly well, all things considered. Bueno is a wonder. He made me drink some stuff last night that tasted like the essence of all the bitterness in the world. But it did the trick. I'm feeling fine."

"I'm very glad," she said simply. "You're returning to Calumet?"

Steve shook his head. "No. I'm going through to Fort Staley. In a few years the country out that way will be opening up. I'm going to have a good look at it as I go along. And if I see a stretch that looks good to me — for cattle, perhaps, I'll plant a couple of claim stakes. I always did have a yen to set my roots in some land no one had ever held before."

Something like relieved eagerness shone in her eyes. "If you are going to Fort Staley, you might just as well travel with us."

Steve shook his head again. "Afraid Maslin wouldn't like that, or those four skinners who don't like my style. They might go temperamental on Race again. Besides, I doubt Ollinger would like me stopping over at his trail stations. So — I'll go it alone."

"But by your own admission — and even

stronger evidence — the Apache roams all through this land," said Lynn. "And with you out there alone — !"

Steve laughed. "I've been alone in bad Apache country before. That doesn't worry me any. But I do hope that you and your brother will see this Apache business in a really practical way from now on. The Apache wouldn't be too concerned about trying to round me up, but they would go all out to raid this wagon train of yours. You see to it that Race never forgets that fact for one moment."

Race came over, leading his own and Lynn's horse. The girl swung up, gave Steve a long, inscrutable look, then said, "Goodby for now, Steve. I hope we'll see you along the trail." Then she reined away.

Race fussed a bit with his saddle, then spoke gruffly. "Dammit, Steve, I wish there was some way to keep you on with us. Frankly, I haven't too much confidence in this fellow Maslin. I don't know whether he's going to prove out or not."

No confidence in Maslin and not too much in yourself, either, thought Steve. Aloud he said, "Race, the middle of a trail is a nice, comfortable place to be. But you can't always stay there, playing both ends against the middle. You can't be all things to all men. In every man's life there come times when he has to take a stand to one side of the trail — and make it stick. About Maslin, if he don't prove out, you still got a good man to take his place. I mean Jake Holcomb. He knows his way about the desert and he knows how to handle men. Well, you better get those wagons rolling. A long day ahead. Good luck, fellah!"

Steve turned and moved away, leading his horse. He stopped by for another moment with Pete Orrick and Bueno, shaking hands. Then he went into the saddle and headed out into the desert.

Slung to his saddle was a gallon canteen of water. In a blanket rolled behind the cantle was a frugal supply of food. He had a rifle under his knee and a Colt at his belt. Under him was a sound, strong horse and ahead of him all the on-running, open miles of the desert, at once a danger and a challenge and a lure. A lightness of spirit, a sense of complete freedom came over Steve. Here were no grinding responsibilities. Here he was on his own.

Several miles out he twisted in the saddle and looked back. A drifting banner of dust lifted back there and under the dust were the wagons, rolling. Out ahead of the wagons rode two tiny figures. Steve knew who these two were — who one in particular was. Lynn.

Some of the lightness of Steve's mood passed. No responsibilities? No contracted ones, perhaps. But there were things back there he could not ride away from completely and know ease of conscience and freedom of heart. For there was no use in denying facts. Such as the warm rush of feeling he had known when Lynn had come up to him this morning, or the way her image persisted in his mind. He didn't know exactly how it had happened, but that slim girl, despite their previous differences, had crept into his consciousness, and there was no forgetting her.

Memory of Hetty Blair came back to him, and he was startled to realize how dim and far away and of little account that memory was now. A shadowy thing, dimming into nothing. But Lynn Ellison, she was vital and real and tremendously important, in a way Hetty Blair had never been. One had been the infatuation produced by a military post's far loneliness and grinding monotony. Based on nothing real, it had never known lasting reality.

But this other — this thing that rode with him now and warmed and stirred him in a deeply vital way, that was based on life's true essences and needs. It was as great as the other had been small.

For the better part of a week Steve Cloud worked his lonely way to the east, riding with sharp alertness all through the day, making frugal camp for the night on some stretch of cap rock, where any restlessness of his horse would bring him fully awake in an instant. It was a trick he had learned from civilian scouts who had ridden with him in his military days.

While working that way east Steve did not hold to a direct line, but made many swings to the north and south, reading the country, constantly on the watch for Apache sign. He saw some, like one little basin in some of the higher country to the north, where a sizable band of Apaches had camped while cooking mescal. But this was old, months old.

It was to the north that he saw country that interested him enough to draw him far that way. It was rising ground, climbing out of the gray and dun and maroon brown of the desert to a wide, running band of tawniness which in turn merged into darker country — country which looked black in some lights and greenish blue in others. Piñon country this, and Steve rode up into it and knew a quickening of spirit as he passed into the first trees.

For a day and a night he camped there beside a small, cold, sweet water creek. Here the air was warm, but it also held an electric keenness, far removed from the lower desert's flat and punishing heat. Here, in meadows scattered through the piñons, was rich grass on which his horse grazed with hungry eagerness. Here a man could live, raise fat cattle, drink sweet water, and know life at its fullest and freest.

And it was here that Steve took the final bandage off his shoulder and left it off. The wound had healed and was only slightly tender to the touch. He could use the arm freely now and the old strength was building up fast. That was this high, dry air, for there was no infection in it. Such poison was reserved for the minds of men. . . .

In a meadow in the piñons he surprised a deer, shot it, hung strips of the meat in the open sun, and this same high, dry air cured it swiftly, and with this provender to augment his other meager food supply, he was set for several more days of solitary wandering. While waiting for the meat to dry and holding to that dream of a ranch in this piñon country, it pleased him to prowl about and select a spot where a headquarters might be built.

He found a place which quickened the

dream — a wide, sloping meadow with that little watercourse droning through it. At its head the meadow flattened, and here would stand the ranch house, log built, and there would be the corrals. Air was constantly stirring in this meadow, flowing up from the far desert, cooling as it climbed, dry and sweet with all the gathered fragrances of space and distance.

Of course, he mused wryly, it was a dream contingent on several factors, not the least of which was the eventual subduing of the Apache threat. But that would come, he knew, in the not-too-distant future. The tide of another race of people was flowing, remorselessly flowing, across this wild southwest country. It was a tide that had begun to move on the far eastern shore of a great continent, working ever on and on toward the sunset land. In its path had been a hundred tribes of Indians who had fought bitterly and valiantly to halt it, and one by one they had been inundated by its swelling power. The Apache was one of the last to go down, but go down they surely would and must.

Many times had Steve Cloud pondered this thing, this on-flowing might of the white man. He had known moments when a strange resentment of it had swayed him, but cooler reflection told him that it was one of those foreordained events in the history of man. It was destiny, inscrutable and, for all he knew, all-wise. No one man, or no one group of men conceived and planned and led a thing so vast and driving. It was the unstoppable flow of life and man's journey to the sun.

As in all such movements in the world's history, it had cost life and blood beyond measure. There had been justice and injustice, there had been honor and perfidy, generosity and greed, friendship and hate. A man, unless he let his thoughts run big, could easily make the mistake of judging it all by the impact it had upon his personal fortunes, when in reality his small affairs counted for very little indeed. It was like an endless column of ants, moving ever onward, impelled by a force they instinctively felt but did not understand. And under the heavy foot of the giant some were crushed and some were spared. . . .

Steve Cloud had never felt the blind hatred for the Apache that some men did. He had fought them, killed some of them, and had known the bite of their arrows in return. He knew they were capable of a ferocity and cruelty that could turn a man inside out. Yet their courage was beyond question, they fought in the only way they knew how, and they fought, as other tribes before them had fought, for what had been theirs down through all the marching centuries.

They fought for their homes and their lands, fought valiantly but hopelessly against a power vast beyond reckoning. And it was a poor man indeed who would not do as much. Their customs, their legends, and they themselves were dying, and their desperate despair was a great and silent cry in the desert night. . . .

Drifting back down to the desert again, Steve Cloud resumed his vigil. Twice he scouted makeshift trail stations that Blake Ollinger had set up, but he did this at a distance, making no attempt to ride into them. He turned to the east, and the mountains that had once loomed so distantly now lifted close, and here the desert began breaking up into low, gaunt hills and rims and ragged gulches. Here also was a faint wagon track leading into this tangled country, and in the late afternoon of one day Steve followed this, deciding that it must lead to the most advanced of Ollinger's stations.

It was just at sundown that his horse began to toss its head and show signs of uneasiness, and only a little later Steve's nostrils twitched at the first grisly stench of death and decay. He slid his rifle from its scabbard and rode slowly on with heightened alertness. And in a small flat beyond a twisting ridge where a water hole showed its seepage he found the dread evidence.

Here had been fire, just blackened embers where once a ramada and corrals had stood. And a wagon, with only its blackened and twisted ironwork showing. Here also were gruesome, bloated things that had once been men and mules, feathered with Apache arrows.

Steve lifted his bleak glance to the upswinging slopes of the barren hills beyond, hills now swimming in the bland deception of the tenderest of powder-blue haze, softened to a strange and wild beauty, but hiding behind that beauty a cruel and mocking danger. Steve turned and rode back the way he had come, his wary glance swinging and searching.

He rode well into the night, until he came to the eastern-most of Ollinger's stations. Here he found four surly, suspicious men. They showed him no welcome nor offer of hospitality, and he wasted no time in gentle language with them. Harshly and bluntly he told them what he had found, and he saw the fear leap into their eyes. They were not the first nor would they be the last to cringe at the word Apache!

Steve Cloud rode again, all the night through, pushing his weary horse without letup. And at sundown of the following day, on a horse almost staggering with exhaustion, and with his own face carved with lines of fatigue and sleeplessness, he rode into Blake Ollinger's Number Three trail station. There he found Race Ellison's wagons drawn up in line but with no mules in evidence.

A slim figure moved out of the shadow of a wagon. It was Lynn Ellison. Under the sun tan her face was drawn and pallid. Her eyes were wide and dark with worry and strain. Steve Cloud swung down, stiff and numb from those piled-up hours in the saddle. He could not keep a thread of harshness from his voice.

"Hello, Lynn. Where's everybody?"

"Our mules are gone," she said tonelessly. "Race and the others are out trying to find them. We've been fools all the way — fools to attempt this thing in the first place — fools to trust men who are fools — !"

Her lips began to work and tremble. Tears were close to spilling over. Steve laid a comforting hand on her arm.

"Steady!" His voice ran more gently. "I don't get this. You say the mules are gone. Gone where? How did it happen?"

She pulled away from his touch. "You left us. You didn't have to. Oh, I know we were stupid enough to put that fool Maslin in your place as wagon boss. But just the same you — you didn't have to leave us —" She dropped her face in her hands and her shoulders began to shake with sobs.

Pete Orrick came prowling out from the wagons. Pete had a rifle in his hands and there was a vast and bitter grimness in his eyes.

"Never was so glad to see a man again," he said harshly. "Somebody had to stay here to keep an eye on things with Miss Lynn, so that's why I'm here. But I ought to be out tryin' to get a line on the mules, because it was my fault that we lost 'em."

"Lost them — how?"

"They were raided, stolen."

"Apaches?"

Pete Orrick shrugged. "I wouldn't know. Whole thing was my fault. I was supposed to be standin' guard and —"

"Standing guard on your own, Pete?" cut in Cloud. "Or under orders from Maslin?"

Pete spat, his leathery face twisting with disgust and anger. "Maslin! That fool never would have sense enough to order out guards. No, it was just me and Bueno, aimin' to do it because we figgered somebody ought to. And it happened durin' my shift. I dozed off somehow. Next I knew the mules were runnin'. I've sure let the folks down, looks like."

"You let nobody down, Pete," said Cloud curtly. "If you weren't under orders to guard, then you're not at fault at all."

Cloud's glance was busy. Down along the row of wagons four men were loafing beside a blanket on which they were playing cards. "The same four," murmured Cloud.

"That's right," growled Pete. "The same damn worthless four. Bascomb an' Jenkins, Hart an' Plank. No good at all, them hombres. If I had my way I'd —"

But Steve Cloud was already moving down on the card-playing quartet. His eyes were full of the dark smoke of bitter anger. He stopped beside the blanket and his voice struck out with the bite of a whip lash.

"On your feet! Get up, you malingering whelps! Here's where you start earning your wages — plenty!"

They stared at him, surly and unresponsive, making no move to obey his order. Jenkins, lank and narrow-faced, sneered and spat.

"Well, if it ain't the little tin ex-soldier, back makin' a big noise again. Now who does he think he is?" Then Jenkins' sneer became an offensive snarl. "You don't rate a thing around this camp, soldier boy. Don't bother us!"

The big Colt gun at Steve's side leaped into his hand, bellowed flatly. The slug smashed into the ground beside Jenkins, spattering him with earth fragments. Jenkins cursed, lunged to his feet, leaped at Steve. And Steve, stepping to meet him, smashed Jenkins across the head with his weapon, dropping the surly teamster in a heap.

The gun swung a slow arc, taking in the other three.

"Get up! On your feet! I don't waste the next bullet on the ground, so don't make the same mistake that fellow did. I've changed my mind about certain things. I started on this trail as wagon boss. Now I'm going to be boss — all the way. I'll kill the next man who tries to flout my authority. You can have it just as rough as you want it. On your feet!"

They got to their feet, shuffling restlessly, and they looked at him before their eyes wavered under the bleak impact of his flat stare. One of them mumbled nervously.

"All right — we're on our feet. Now what do we do?"

"Why, you go to work," lashed Steve.

"Any work, any chore, whether it needs doing or not. One thing is dead certain. You're all through lazing around, grousing over this and that. For a starter you can grease wagons. And you do a job of it — a real job. Pete, you see that they do just that. If they try to shirk, work them over with the butt of your gun. And before you tie into a grease bucket, you" — and he stabbed a finger at one of them — "you take care of my horse. Unsaddle it, water and feed it, and give it a real rubdown. For it's a good horse, worth a million like you. Try to buck me, any of you, and you'll never see Fort Staley or Calumet either. You'll stay right here, six feet under. Get going!"

Pete Orrick dropped his rifle over his arm. "Now," he said, with huge satisfaction, "now we're gettin' somewhere. Now we're comin' to common sense. You jiggers heard your orders. Start workin'!"

They did, plainly shaken and fearful. Jenkins lay right as he had dropped, still motionless. Steve Cloud looked at him for a moment, then turned back to Lynn Ellison, who had watched and listened to it all.

"So I'm brutal again," he said. "But have you got a better answer?"

Her tears were gone. Her eyes were dry and her face stoic. "I'll not question your

173

purpose or methods again," she said tone-lessly. Then she turned and walked away.

Moving stiffly, Cloud got a bucket of water and sluiced the unconscious Jenkins with it. The fellow stirred, groaned, got to one elbow, blear-eyed and sick. He got no sympathy from Cloud, who urged him along with a none-too-gentle boot toe.

"On your feet! There's work to do. Pete, take him over and put him at greasing wagons if he has to spread the grease with his face. We're through fooling around."

Steve Cloud turned away.

Jenkins had to try three times before he could get his feet under him and keep them there. Pete Orrick, watching him grimly, said, "So now you know, my fine bucko. There'll be no back talk."

It was well after deep dark had fallen before Race Ellison came riding in, glum and discouraged. With him were Bueno, griz-zled Jake Holcomb, Blake Ollinger, and Maslin. Bueno, seeing Steve Cloud hun-kered down wearily beside a fire, came swiftly over to him, his black eyes shining.

"This is good, señor," he said simply, "to see you with us again. I hope it is to stay?"

"It is," said Pete Orrick, from across the fire. "And there's four plumb new educated hombres who realize it — plenty!"

"The mules, Bueno — what about them?" asked Steve.

Bueno shrugged. "We did not come up with them. At first we thought an Apache raid would follow the thievery, so we did not leave the wagons at once. We lost time and the mules were far, far ahead by the time we started after them. Of only two things I am certain, Señor Steve. White men, not Apaches, stole the mules. And they drive them back toward the river, from the way we come."

"Toward the river, eh?" murmured Steve. "Toward Calumet. So that could be —"

"Fallon and Overgaard," cut in Race Ellison, coming up out of the gloom. Race was harsh, weary, plainly discouraged. He stood looking down at Steve Cloud.

"I've been the biggest damn fool in the world," he went on bluntly. "I let my common sense and judgment be upset by four worthless whelps of mule skinners — and by others. Steve, I'm eating the coldest of cold crow right now. I want you back at your old job. I'll pay you double if you'll come. I want no more of such as Maslin. He's only a stage less fool than I've been. And Blake Ollinger — well, he'll have to understand the desert a lot better than he does now if he expects to make a success of that trail-station idea of his. I confess I'm about licked. I'm afraid to advance an idea, because I've been so wrong before. Will you take over, Steve? Name your own price and I'll do my best to meet it."

"We won't worry about that just now," said Steve quietly. "We've other things of more importance to settle. Where's Ollinger? I've some bad news for him."

Race Ellison turned and called into the darkness, his voice abrupt and harsh. "Ollinger! Come here!"

Presently Ollinger came up to the fire, his eyes wary and unreadable, his manner stiffly hostile.

"Steve Cloud's got something to say to you," said Race. "When he's done I've a word or two of my own."

Ollinger shrugged and growled. "I'm listening."

"You're supposed to be setting up trail stations between Calumet and Fort Staley," said Steve evenly. "That's what the deal was between you and the Ellisons, wasn't it?"

"You're camped at one right now," retorted Ollinger. "Need further proof?"

"Depends on what you call a trail station," drawled Steve. "My definition of a trail station on which a wagon train could

176

depend for safety and supply is vastly different than these places of yours. Some of yours I've seen a dozen Apaches could wipe off the map without raising a sweat."

"What Apaches?" The tone and words were insolent, sneering.

Steve Cloud straightened to his feet, stared hard at Ollinger. "You figured on setting up one station out at the foot of those humpbacked hills way over east?"

"Not figured on it. I have set one up. I got men out there right now. I'm way ahead of you, mister."

Steve shook his head. "No, you're not. You haven't got any station out there."

Ollinger rocked up on his toes. "What are you driving at? What do you mean — I haven't got a station out there?"

"I've been doing quite a bit of scouting since I saw you last, Ollinger," Steve said curtly. "I saw wagon tracks leading in there, so I thought I'd have a look. I found what was left of a burned wagon and ramada and corrals. I found dead men and dead mules full of Apache arrows. It wasn't very pretty. So now you know."

"That's a long way west for Apaches to strike in force," rasped Ollinger, half-doubting.

Steve shrugged. "All I know is what I've

told you. The men are dead, the mules are dead, and the rest burned. The buzzards and coyotes had already been busy. You're welcome to the information, but I don't give a thin damn whether you want to believe it or not."

Ollinger stared at the flames for a time, his face sullen. Then he turned to Race Ellison. "You got something on your mind?"

"Considerable," shot back Race. "Maslin is through. You can tell him so for me. If he's a wagon boss, I'm the emperor of China. I don't know what I'm going to do about mules. But if and when I do manage to round up enough to haul my wagons, this is to be understood. While my wagon train is in camp at any of your stations, what my wagon boss says — goes! If he says guards are to be posted, they'll be posted — and everybody will do his part."

"With Maslin out — you got a wagon boss?" There was a taunt in Ollinger's tone.

"Yeah," said Steve Cloud. "He has. Me. For keeps this time."

Ollinger looked at Race Ellison again. "If the way my trail stations are run don't suit you, you don't have to camp at them, you know."

"But I will," flared Race, "because there is where the best water will be. So I'll camp there, whether you like it or not. You don't own the water, so never make the mistake of thinking you can keep me away from it. I've listened to several of your ideas in the past and so far none of them have been sound. From now on I'm relying completely on the advice and judgment of one man. Steve Cloud. If I'd listened to him in the first place I wouldn't be stranded here minus mules."

Race and Ollinger matched hard glances. And it was Ollinger whose glance shifted. He whirled and stamped away. Race stared after him for a moment, then turned to Steve.

"If you got any suggestions about the mules," he said wearily, "I'll be glad to hear them."

"Get something to eat, first," Steve advised. "Then we'll see what we can figure out. I'll want your sister in on the talk too. For the time has come to make some pretty important decisions, and once they're made this time, they'll have to stand, come hell or high water."

8

Pausing only long enough to gulp some food and saddle fresh horses, Ollinger and Maslin headed east into the desert toward the next trail station. This the soft-footed, watchful Bueno reported to Steve Cloud.

"He didn't like the news you brought, Señor Steve. But he believed you, after all."

Race and Lynn Ellison came up to Steve's fire shortly after and sat there. The girl was still-faced, brooding, staring at the flames. Race's mood was little different.

"First about the mules," began Steve. "Bueno declares that white men pulled the raid and I'm sure he's right. I'm equally certain that Fallon and Overgaard are responsible because that fits in with a lot of other angles. We'll take steps to get those mules back, of course, but first there are some other decisions to be made." A somewhat harsh finality came into Steve's tone which caused Race Ellison to study him intently.

"I can't think of any decision more important than getting the mules back. What are you driving at?"

"You heard what I said to Ollinger about his trail stations," explained Steve. "Good enough, perhaps in peaceful country, but next to worthless in real Apache territory. And that's what lies ahead now — between here and Fort Staley. I find it hard to understand the man — Ollinger, I mean. Either he is a complete fool, trying to throw up flimsy stations, undermanned and poorly protected, or he has some sort of scheme in mind that isn't all it should be. In short, from what I've seen of them up ahead we'd be feeble-witted to depend on Ollinger's stations for anything except the water there. From here on, once we get rolling again" — and now he let his grave glance swing around the listening circle — "we're going to have to fight our way through — on our own. The danger is going to be great. Believe me I'm not magnifying that in the slightest. So the question is — do you want to go on, Race?"

"Go on? Of course. What else is there to do?"

Steve Cloud shrugged. "Think on it, Race — you and your sister. So far your wagons and their loads are safe. But the day we roll out of this camp, heading east, that safety becomes a gamble. Out there in the desert you could lose everything. So far our Apache trouble has been virtually negligible. But it's going to be terribly real before we ever see Fort Staley. Real enough to wipe you out. Here you can turn back. Out there, once you're committed, that chance will be gone."

Race shifted restlessly. "If we don't go on — and get through — our contract with the Army will be gone. And we've gambled everything on that contract."

"You'd still have your wagons — your outfits. You could probably pick up some other freighting business closer to the river, in comparatively safe country. You'd still have something."

Now it was Lynn Ellison who spoke. "You're trying to discourage us. Why now?"

"Not discourage you," corrected Steve quietly, "but to have you thoroughly understand the facts. I never did minimize the danger, did I? Yet at one time I believed we'd have some help from Ollinger. Now I know we won't — not enough help to count. That's the point I want to put over. From here on we can depend on nothing but our own efforts — and from here on is where the trail gets really rough. It's your decision — yours and Race's. Be sure it's the right one, for there'll be no chance of changing it once we roll again."

She searched his face carefully. "If the wagons were yours, the contract yours, and the conditions the same — what would you do?"

"They're not my wagons and the decision isn't mine," he evaded. "This is strictly up to you and Race."

She understood his wariness. "We deserve that answer, Race and I do. We've been foolish and unjust in several things. The blame for our troubles is all our own. We both admit that frankly. Now may I have an answer?"

Steve stared with narrowed eyes at the flames, then nodded. "Very well. If the layout was mine and the contract mine, I'd recognize the danger fully. And then I'd go on. I'd make the try for Fort Staley."

"Then," said Lynn Ellison, "Race and I will do the same. We will go on."

"That's right." Race nodded. "We'll go on." He added wryly, "But there's a little question of mules first. What about them, Steve?"

"We'll get mules," said Cloud. "We'll get them from the men who stole ours. First thing in the morning Pete, Bueno, Jake Holcomb, and myself start back for the river — after mules. You'll stay here, Race, to

183

keep an eye on things. I think Jenkins and those other three skinners have pretty well learned their lesson now. If they haven't, don't hesitate to work them over. Make them understand that they hired on to run a jerk line as far as Staley and back, and that we intend seeing to it that they do, if we have to scatter their bones along the way. Keep them busy. See that they stand guard every night. Be the boss all the way. If necessary, throw a gun on them. And — keep an eye on Ollinger and all his doings."

Race stirred restlessly. "Does that last add up, Steve?"

"I think so. In the desert a smart man watches everything and everybody."

Race and Lynn Ellison moved away from the fire slowly. The girl, her face shadowed, looked back. Steve Cloud was staring off into the night as though, despite the dark, he had vision to see things far off and invisible to others. The marks of his hard riding were on him, gaunting him, pulling the weather-blackened skin taut across the flat planes of his face, and his eyes were deep with shadow.

Abruptly, despite the loss of the mules, the crushed despair that had been over Lynn now suddenly lifted. The future, which had seemed so hopeless, now showed new light and promise. And all because this one man had returned to camp.

She carried the picture of him, there beside the fire, up to her last moment of wakefulness that night.

They were up and gone while the stars were still bright in the morning sky. Four of them. Steve Cloud and Bueno, Pete Orrick, and crusty, dependable Jake Holcomb.

Steve led the way, heading due west and setting a fast pace to make the most of the cool hours before sunup. There had not been enough horses to fit them all with fresh mounts, but Steve had this angle figured. They would make a change of animals at Blake Ollinger's Number Two station.

Thinking as he rode, Steve saw with a quickening clarity the logic of holding Fallon and Overgaard responsible for the loss of the mules. It was the only answer that made sense. They had already made a couple of fruitless tries at stalling the Ellison wagons. They'd tried to hire Steve away from the Ellisons and when they failed in that had turned Jess Brokaw loose on him, figuring that Brokaw would maul him to such a stage of physical helplessness he'd be unable to make the trip. But this had backfired.

So now Fallon and Overgaard had struck

185

with much greater shrewdness and effect. They had left the Ellison wagons helpless far out in the desert. Calumet was days away and a satisfactory source of supply for more mules still farther distant. Trying to round up another supply of animals through regular channels could mean a delay of weeks. So, Steve told himself, he wouldn't consider those channels unless there was no other out. Instead, he'd play the game now according to the rules Fallon and Overgaard had written. For in this part of the world, it seemed, a man had to make his own law as he went along. It might be brigand or outlaw rule, but it had to do.

They rode the early-morning hours out, felt the first bite of a new sun between their shoulders, kept their horses to a driving pace. What with their early start, and covering ground at a far faster pace than a loaded wagon could roll, they reached Blake Ollinger's Number Two station by midday.

Ollinger's stationmaster there was bullet-headed and surly, and not at all sympathetic with Steve Cloud's needs, flatly refusing to exchange fresh horses for the jaded animals Steve and his companions rode in on. He claimed, with rough bluster, that he had no authority from Ollinger to make such an exchange, and until he did have, wouldn't

186

swap horses with any man.

Steve heard the fellow through, his eyes darkening and pinching down. Then he turned to the others.

"Pick out the best ones," he ordered curtly.

The stationmaster cursed and put his back to the corral gate. "Why, damn your gall! I said no go, and that's what I mean. The first man who touches — !"

That was as far as he got before Steve grabbed him, spun him away from the gate, and slammed him against the corral fence. Steve's words crackled.

"You make a pass for your gun and I take it away from you and make you eat it! We need those horses and we're taking them. Stay wide!"

The fellow gulped and backed away from what he saw in Steve's eyes.

They rode the afternoon out, cutting down the miles rapidly on the fresh mounts. At dusk they unsaddled for a short rest and a frugal bite to eat. They grained their horses on a ration of precious oats taken from Blake Ollinger's station bin, then set saddles again and pushed on through the night.

As they rode, Steve explained his strategy to his companions. Once the raiders were

assured that they had outdistanced immediate pursuit, he reasoned, they would slack
their pace. The raiders might scatter the
mules and leave them to the desert to take
care of, but this was doubtful. For along this
frontier mules were a valuable commodity,
and men like Fallon and Overgaard, lawless
enough to have pulled the raid in the first
place, were hardly likely to throw away the
profit that lay in the animals. They might
not head directly back to Calumet with
them, but they would hit the river either up
or down stream and sell the mules there.
Again, they might throw the animals in with
their own herd and use them. For there was
no law of any real moment along this part of
the frontier and no one to call Fallon and
Overgaard to account save the man or men
they had robbed.

Therefore, Steve said, if they could reach
the river ahead of the stolen mules, they
would be in a position to pull a surprise on
the thieves, who would never expect them
there, but who would, instead, be watching
their back trail.

They passed Ollinger's Number One station during the night, swinging by within
half a mile of it. They kept their horses
steadily to the chore and night's coolness
enabled the animals to give of their best.

And so it was, in a dawn laced with mists from the river which lay below, they looked down on a sleeping Calumet from the first low rise where the desert climbed to the east.

They scouted the town before it was fully awake, and Steve sent Pete Orrick and Bueno down to the wagon camp and corrals along the river to see how things were there. Bueno's black eyes were gleaming with excitement when he and Pete returned.

"Plenty of mules there, Señor Steve," Bueno reported. "Not our mules, but those of Fallon and Overgaard. Fat, well-rested mules. I was thinking, señor — we exchanged horses along the trail. Why not exchange mules — Fallon and Overgaard mules — for those they stole from us?"

"Bueno's right, boy." Pete Orrick nodded. "The mules down there all carry Fallon and Overgaard's Crescent brand. We're either here ahead of the stolen herd, or, like you said they might, the raiders are bringing them into the river somewhere up or down stream. About Bueno's idea, I can't see a thing wrong with it."

"Nor me," growled crusty Jake Holcomb. "Take what we need and let Fallon and Overgaard figger out the next move."

A hot, raw recklessness was surging in

189

Steve Cloud's veins. There had been a time in his life when what Bueno and Pete and Jake proposed would have been met with blunt, stern refusal. Now he was amazed at the way the precise rulings of his past military service were being completely and rapidly shucked from his shoulders. In those days a man lived utterly to preordained rulings, to an ironbound and inflexible code of thought and behavior. Steve had never questioned the rightness nor necessity of this code, for it served successfully the ends of the Army, and the Army was all that counted.

Different now. Then, when a man wanted something, or needed it for a necessary purpose, he secured it through requisition routed in set and settled channels. But now all was different. A man won or lost, succeeded or failed, even lived or died, it seemed, by his ability to strike back as he had been struck, meet ruthlessness with even greater ruthlessness. Here, military law and protocol were supplanted by the oldest and most fundamental law of a wild frontier. Survival of the fit — of the strong. An eye for an eye . . . ! It went back into the dimmest pages of written history.

Steve shook himself. "We'll think about it," he said. "But we got to remember there's

190

only the four of us, and we won't help our cause any by jumping into something before we know how we'll land. We'll look into things a little first."

They were the first customers of the morning at a tawdry hash house, and they ate ravenously. After which they rode down to the wagon camp and looked the setup over at a distance. Half-a-dozen shuffling roustabouts were in evidence, caring for the mules, watering and feeding them.

"Nothing to worry about there," said Pete Orrick. "One shot over their heads an' they'll run for cover. Let's go in an' help ourselves."

Steve shook his head. "Not too fast, Pete. Taking the mules would be simple enough perhaps, but getting them out to where our wagons are would be something else again, what with Fallon and Overgaard pounding our trail with a bunch of tough ones. We can't afford to make any mistakes in this. We got to work out the surest way."

Bueno hissed softly. "Yonder, Señor Steve. Past those wagons. Grimes Fallon and Hack Overgaard!"

Steve looked and saw the lank, tight-featured, pale-eyed Fallon and the hulking Overgaard. They had been down beyond the wagons somewhere and now they came

191

out into the clear. A glint flickered in Steve's eyes.

"Maybe we've got a break of luck here. You fellows stay put unless things turn rough."

Steve rode down toward the corrals, angling to come up with Fallon and Overgaard. He had no idea how things might work out but was certain of one thing. To win anything in this game a man had to play his hand boldly.

Fallon and Overgaard spotted him, exchanged some kind of comment, watched him ride up, in their eyes the light of mockery and smug triumph. And if Steve Cloud had known any doubt before, he would have been certain now that these two were responsible for the raid on Race Ellison's mules. Steve returned their glances stonily.

Grimes Fallon spat, revolved a cud of tobacco in his mouth, spat again. "If you've come back to take us up on our offer of a job, Cloud, you can forget it. We're just not interested any more in you. Or maybe that ain't the reason you've come draggin' back here to Calumet. Maybe Ellison has run into a little difficulty out along the trail, eh?"

Hack Overgaard's laugh was a hoarse blurting. "You know, Cloud, Grimes an' me, we tried to tell Ellison he wasn't a big enough freight operator to handle that government contract. But he's a smart hombre, Elison is, in his own estimation — an' bullheaded. One of those guys too wise for their own good. An' his kind always end up bogged in trouble."

Words now, thought Steve, with poorly veiled inferences to mock him. An answering anger ran coldly through him. But he kept it locked behind inscrutable features. They were, he concluded, absolutely sure of their ground. They liked the cards they held, for they figured them the highest.

Steve doubted the two of them were personally present at the raid; they did not have the look of recent hard riding across the desert. But it was plain they'd received word of the raid and of its success. Steve's glance became a flat stare, measuring the pair of them coldly.

"Yeah," he admitted, "Race Ellison did run into trouble. Mule trouble. Some damn dirty thieves raided him and ran off his animals. Which fact you two know all about, seeing you're directly responsible. So now I've come back here to make a few adjustments. With the pair of you. Personally."

"Well now," said Fallon with obvious relish, "I can't think of a thing you can do

193

that'll help Ellison except ride back to him and tell him that Hack an' me will buy him out. We'll take his wagons an' other gear — plus that government contract — off his hands. At our price, of course. Now we think that's a real fair sort of deal, don't we, Hack?"

Came Overgaard's hoarse, blurting laugh again. "Fair as hell, Grimes."

Up from somewhere deep inside of Steve Cloud came a raw and swelling hatred of these two. Gloating, leering, ruthless — smug with the success of their plans. It meant not a thing to them that the garrison at Fort Staley might be badly in need of the supplies lying out there in the desert in Race Ellison's stalled wagons. Part of those supplies, Steve knew, was ammunition. Troopers in the uniform of their country, men faced with the hardest kind of campaigning against a remorseless foe of unparalleled ferocity and cunning, might die because of lack of those supplies.

But Grimes Fallon and Hack Overgaard did not give a thin damn about this. Their only concern was their own idea of profits and to hell with the lengths they had to go to secure such. The welfare of the very men who kept the Apache threat away from these two and their freighting operations meant nothing to them. They were no better than brigands and deserved no more consideration.

The black anger deepened in Steve Cloud and he threw his decision at them in curt and brittle words.

"Your crowd pulled a smart raid. They got all of Race Ellison's mules. Maybe you think that fills your hands with winning cards. You're wrong. It doesn't. For I'm here to make a swap. For every mule you stole from us I'm taking one of those animals of yours. Nice-looking mules you got here. Good condition, rested, ready to haul our wagons the rest of the way to Fort Staley. Now you know!"

It seemed to take a long moment for the full import of Steve's declaration to strike home. It was as though these two, Fallon and Overgaard, were so sure of their ground that Steve's words were of no concern to them whatever.

"You are," flayed Steve, "a pair of damned, dirty, crooked thieves!"

This harsh emphasis bit deep. Fallon pulled his lank length up tautly, his thin face twisting in a dark flush. But it was Overgaard, full-fledged brute that he was, who really reacted. He whirled fully to face Steve, a big hairy fist brushing suggestively past the gun at his hip.

"Why, you sniveling pup of an ex-tin soldier, who do you think you're talkin' to? Who do you expect to bluff or scare with that kind of talk? I've heard all the story about you — why they kicked you out of the Army. For being a damned coyote — that's why they did it. Because you turned yellow and ran out on a supply train you were supposed to guard. Yeah, I heard all that from Blake Ollinger. Blake told Grimes an' me —"

"Hack, you damned fool!" yelled Fallon. "Shut up! You want — ?"

"So that's it," cut in Steve Cloud. He was smiling coldly. "I had the hunch all along. You two and Blake Ollinger — three snakes in the same basket. Now that will interest Race Ellison. And the Army, when they hear about it, as they will. Race Ellison trying sincerely and honestly to fulfill his contract with them, while you three were scheming all the time — Well, well. Wait until the Army does hear about it. I know what they'll think, I know what they'll say, I know what they'll do. I prophesy that this southwest territory will become very unhealthy for you two and for Mister Blake Ollinger — oh, very! Why, the lowest Apache, full of tiswin beer and animal ferocity, is a complete gentleman alongside three whelps like you fellows — a very complete gentleman!"

In the unthinking wave of his arrogance Hack Overgaard had said far more than he intended. For him and Fallon to fight Race Ellison for a government hauling contract, regardless of tactics employed, was one thing, and might have been condoned. But by ringing in Blake Ollinger on the deal, that amounted to conspiracy against the very real interests of the government. And the government was known to deal harshly with those who conspired against it.

There was a fine legal distinction here which Hack Overgaard could recognize though not fully understand in all its ramifications. His part knowledge and part ignorance in the matter were worse than knowing everything or knowing nothing at all. And because he was the sort of person he was he could think of only one way of stopping what his unthinking words had started. And that was to still forever the ears that had heard his damaging admission.

Steve Cloud, razor-sharp alert, saw the feral, desperate purpose take form in Overgaard's eyes, and he moved to meet it as fast and as savagely as it came to him. He dropped flat along the neck of his horse, dragging at his holstered gun as he did so.

He saw Overgaard's gun flick out and up. Then the heavy bellow of the weapon pounded his ears, and a spreading gout of smoke lashed in his face.

As he drew, Hack Overgaard had fixed his target, which was the center of Steve Cloud's chest as Steve sat his saddle with a cavalryman's trained erectness. But when Steve dropped along the neck of his horse, Overgaard's reflexes were not swift enough to meet the flashing change. His slug went where Steve had been, not where he was now. Hack Overgaard missed — overshot at fifteen-foot range.

Into the gushing smoke Steve Cloud drove two bullets in return. He gigged his horse sharply, lifting it into a wide, plunging leap to one side. He threw another shot and saw Overgaard's hulking figure collapse. Again Steve used the spurs, and this time his horse lunged straight at Grimes Fallon who, stunned by Overgaard's sudden, wild break, was slow in his instinctive dodge. The hurtling shoulder of Steve Cloud's horse smashed into him, knocking him spinning. And when Fallon, cursing and gasping, scrambled dizzily to his feet, he found himself under the grim muzzle of Steve Cloud's gun.

"If you want it," gritted Steve, "you can

have it. Otherwise, get your hands up!"

Fallon's hands lifted shakily. His head swung and he looked down at Hack Overgaard's sprawled and violence-distorted figure. Overgaard was quite dead, an ominous stain seeping from a bullet hole through the base of his throat. Fallon shivered as though icy cold and he licked his lips, and when his head came up again his narrow face had gone pallid and greasy with the sweat of pure fear.

"The game, you see," said Steve, softly bleak, "grows rough. Those hands — get them a little higher!"

Down from where they had been watching raced Bueno, Jake Holcomb, and Pete Orrick. Steve said, "Now we'll take the mules we need." His gun made a little dipping motion toward Grimes Fallon. "And we take him along as a hostage to guarantee that we keep them. Bueno, look him over for a gun."

The roustabouts caring for the Fallon and Overgaard mules had been too busy to pay much attention to the meeting of their bosses with Steve Cloud and too distant to note the words that had passed between them. But the sudden, eruptive booming of the guns brought them all whirling and moving with alarm. What they now saw sent the more timid scurrying to places of shelter, while the nervier ones edged up in a surly and threatening group.

"Watch those!" ordered Steve sharply, and this Jake Holcomb and Pete Orrick and Bueno immediately did. Holcomb sent his hard and crusty voice winging across the corrals and wagon park.

"Keep clear! No trouble for you if you do, but plenty of it if you don't. Keep clear!"

They obeyed only in part. They came no closer at the moment but Steve Cloud could see that feeling was rising steadily and cementing the hardier ones into something that could cause plenty of trouble. So he looked across his gun at Grimes Fallon.

"You! Tell 'em to cool off. You're their boss. Hurry up — tell 'em!"

Fallon seemed relieved to find an outlet for his numbed feelings. His voice lifted shrilly as he ordered his roustabouts back, cursing one or two of the more reluctant ones. Steve saw one burly fellow shrug his shoulders and heard him say, "Fallon's pie, looks like. Let him eat it."

This threat taken care of, Steve questioned Fallon. "Where were our mules taken to?"

"Spice Mountain."

"Upriver or down — and how far?"

"Up. Fifteen miles about."

200

"Too far to go after them and a bunch of worn-out animals when we get there," said Steve. "So we trade. One of yours for every one of ours. Order your men to bring them out and bunch them for us. Holcomb, you know mules. See that we get only the best ones."

Grimes Fallon's first sweating terror was fading. A small thread of bluster came into his words.

"This is the most high-handed — ! Cloud, you can't get away with this. I won't — !"

Steve swung off his horse, locked his free left hand in the front of Fallon's shirt, shoved him back a step or two.

"You'll do exactly as you're told to do, mister. You couldn't make a worse mistake than to think I won't skin you and hang your hide up to dry if you try to go stubborn on me. Not only for what you've done and are trying to do to Race Ellison, but because of a personal reason. You think I've forgotten that night in Calumet when Jess Brokaw jumped me? That big, mauling animal! I had to club him down like a mad dog, to keep him from crippling or killing me."

Steve's grip tightened and he gave Fallon another backward shove. "Why did Brokaw jump me? Not of his own accord, for he didn't know me from Adam, had never seen

201

me before. Why did a bunch of river toughs try to club my brains out down at the Pomo landing? You know, Fallon — you know damn well why. Because you and Overgaard set Brokaw after me and it was Ollinger who was behind that river tough gang attack at Pomo. The idea was to cripple me up or kill me, so I couldn't take on with the Ellisons. That's the answer, isn't it? Well, when you write the rules of a game, Fallon, they work both ways. Now you know!"

All bluster ran out of Grimes Fallon. By now Steve had him backed up against a corral fence — hard! And the cold blaze in Steve's eyes was too much for him. He nodded again and again his admission to Steve's charges. He gulped. "Just as you say — it's like you say — !"

It did not take very long to get the mules out of the corrals and lined up. Grimes Fallon gave out the orders that Steve told him to give. With lengths of rope Jake Holcomb worked out an ingenious hitch, which tethered the mules together in three strings. Several animals which the roustabouts brought out Holcomb turned back, demanding better ones. In the end, only the soundest and best-conditioned animals made up the strings.

A horse for Fallon was ordered out and

saddled. Then Steve Cloud looked at the burly roustabout who seemed to be in some authority over the rest.

"These mules are in exchange for a like number which Fallon and Overgaard ordered stolen from Race Ellison. Maybe you know about that, maybe you don't. Either way, those are the facts. Don't try to organize any pursuit, or to interfere in any way with us again. If you do — it's Fallon's neck." He turned to Fallon. "You want to add anything to that?"

It was plain that there were any number of things which Grimes Fallon would have liked to say and do. But it was also plain that he recognized a complete checkmate all along the line. His glance went again to Hack Overgaard. "What about — him?" he blurted.

"Big country," countered Steve harshly. "Far better men than Hack Overgaard have been buried in it. Now we start!"

Jake Holcomb took the lead, with Pete Orrick and Bueno following in that order. Each of them had a long string of mules at lead. Steve jerked a curt head. "Now you, Fallon. I don't like your kind riding at my back."

There was a cold rigidity along Steve's spine that did not leave until they were beyond long rifle shot from the wagon camp and corrals. Then he let out a long, slow breath and relaxed somewhat.

Those had been tight moments back there. He had played a bold and reckless hand, and that very boldness, plus a big slice of luck, had put it over. How Hack Overgaard had ever missed him he'd never know. Alert as he had been and, just before the break, fully conscious of what Hack Overgaard was going to attempt, Steve knew he had been behind Overgaard at the start and his own moves had been instinctive and desperate. And Overgaard had missed, and he hadn't.

He thought of how Hack Overgaard had looked, sprawled there in death, and a cold thickness crawled around in his stomach and pushed up in his throat. It wasn't the first time Steve Cloud had looked at violent death. He had known, perhaps, more than his share of the hot and fetid breath of desperate battle against the Apache. Men had died beside him, comrades in arms, some in swift, stricken silence and some in haggard agony. Over the sights of his own gun he had seen more than one of the enemy collapse into stillness.

But that was battle, where men lived and died in high fury that was strangely impersonal. This affair with Hack Overgaard was different, vastly so. Here had been no justifying military action or order. Here had been merely gun fight, raw and savage and deadly. Man to man. Kill or be killed. And Steve Cloud was now queerly shaken as he recalled the swift swelling ferocity with which he had struck back.

This was what the desert did to a man when he fought for his own fortunes and purposes. When the smoke of a battlefield had cleared and the totals cast up, the written record took care of the results and all men were absolved from individual responsibility, and duty went on and a man could forget. But this other — !

Steve's mood darkened as he rode. In a man's youth, it seemed, life had thunder in it and moments of wild fury. Steve wondered if, with the maturity of added years, would come forgetting.

9

At Blake Ollinger's Station Three the days were empty and bitter for Lynn and Race Ellison. The nights were long and still, full of the nameless threat of a wild desert which neither of them had fully understood but of which they were now gleaning understanding the hard way.

They had known the country along the river, but that was a path which men were traveling with increasing frequency. Such as it was, there at least was a fringe of civilization that held a reasonable security for the individual and his plans and activities. But out here — !

Race Ellison now carried a gun with him constantly. He carried also an entirely new and hardening concept of realities. With the four recalcitrant skinners, Jenkins, Hart, Bascomb, and Plank, he was grim and blunt and uncompromising. Throughout all the day he kept them busy, cleaning harness, checking wagons and loads, even if they had to do the same job over and over again. And at night they stood guard shifts and they stayed awake and alert, for Race checked them closely. He told them bluntly that they would do as they were told, with no back talk, or he would use the gun he carried. The bitter truths of the desert were working on Race and he was learning. Yet he knew a harsh satisfaction in the realization that his stature of capability was increasing.

It was hardest on Lynn Ellison. The heat, the monotony, the gnawing uncertainty of the future, these things were at work on her and bringing about a dismal subduing of spirit. It was not reasonable to expect that she would toughen up as fast as her brother. Race recognized his sister's problems, but there was nothing he could do beyond a declared optimism for the future.

"So far we've lost nothing but time," he told her. "And I'm certain that the authorities at Fort Staley will be lenient with us there. For, after all, with this first trip we are setting up a brand-new supply line. It was too much to expect that the initial try would go through smoothly. They'll understand that, Lynn, and make allowances."

"Only time?" retorted Lynn. "How about our mules?"

"One ties in with the other," asserted Race stoutly. "And I'm through doubting

Steve Cloud in any way. He said he'd bring those mules back, or replace them, and I'm going to believe him. Such things take time and we've got to be patient."

Patience. A person had to acquire it in deepest meaning here in the desert or go all to pieces. For the desert was old, old beyond counting, and time, as men measured it, meant nothing to the desert. Yes, there had to be patience and stoicism.

These things Lynn considered with brooding thought as she would sit in the shade of a wagon and watch the everlasting sun beat up writhing heat devils across the barren miles. And much of her watching was out across the mocking emptiness to the west.

The desert had changed her physically. It had thinned her face and darkened her skin. It had thrown violence before her and some terror and had shown her the make-up of men. There was, she mused, a vast difference in the fiber a man might show under reasonably pleasant and comfortable circumstances and what he would be under opposite conditions. That was the desert again. It stripped off thin veneer and showed the dubious quality of the real wood underneath.

Like Blake Ollinger, for instance. He had

returned from his visit to his Station Four and from further journey to the foot of the humpbacked hills to the east. What he had found there had left him morose for a day or two. The flair, the dash, the swagger he had displayed along the river were missing now. He and Race had had one session of angry words and then avoided each other.

Late one afternoon Ollinger sought out Lynn where she rested beside a wagon, her slim shoulders braced against the spokes of a mighty wheel. He dropped down beside her and spoke abruptly.

"This desert is no place for you, Lynn. You should never have come along. You should have stayed in Calumet."

Lynn looked at him impassively. "So Steve Cloud tried to tell me. But where Race and the wagons go, I go."

She saw a hot flicker jump into Ollinger's eyes at mention of Steve Cloud. Ollinger felt her glance and looked away. He switched the subject abruptly.

"If Race is smart, he'll give up this government contract. He isn't organized to carry it through. Once I thought he was, but I can see now that he's not. He was doing all right freighting to the mines down around Ehrenberg. But the setup was far different there than it is here. Things have piled up on him. He's definitely stalled. His mules are gone, men he mistakenly trusted are gone. I very much doubt he'll ever see them again, men or mules. No, I can't see any success for him in this venture."

"How about yourself?" retorted Lynn. "Are your affairs doing so well?"

Ollinger shrugged. "I'll make out. My deal isn't tied in with the fulfilling of a government contract. I'm not up against a time limit. I can afford to have setbacks and delays. You and Race can't."

The warmth of spirit glowed briefly in Lynn's cheeks. "Race and I are far from whipped. We'll not give up our contract with the government. The future is too big. We'll get more mules and our wagons will roll again. Race believes it, I believe it, and Steve Cloud believes it."

Blake Ollinger made a hard cutting motion with his hand. "Steve Cloud! That fellow's smooth. Oh, I admit he took me in at first. I thought he had the stuff you and Race needed. But now — ! Lynn, I've been remembering something about Steve Cloud — and thinking about it. That afternoon at your wagon camp at Calumet — remember? What did you and Race and I run across that time? Why, Mister Steve having deep talk with Grimes Fallon and Hack Overgaard.

What, I wonder, were they talking about?"

"Steve explained that to us," answered Lynn, a little sharply. "You were there and heard him. Fallon and Overgaard had been trying to hire him away from Race and me, and he had turned them down flat."

"So he said. But in light of things that have happened since — well, I'm wondering. Because I remember other things. I remember that he was kicked out of the Army. Why? The story, as I've heard it, was because he lost his nerve and deserted a wagon train he was supposed to guard, and left that train to the Apaches. That may be all of the story or only part of it. But one thing is certain. The army does not court-martial an officer and drum him out of service in disgrace without good and sufficient reason. So there you have the man in whom you and Race are putting your trust and all the future of your freighting project. Doubtful hands, my dear — oh, very doubtful hands."

For a little time Lynn was silent, inwardly shaken. She sensed a glibness in Ollinger's tone, but there were some undeniable facts in his words, though facts which could be construed in different ways. Protest rose in her, and a certain defiance. You had to believe in something, in someone.

"I'm believing there are two sides to everything," she declared. "So there is Steve's side to his trouble in the Army. We haven't heard that yet. And he seems to have the knack of attracting to his side the best men in our outfit. Men like Bueno and Pete Orrick and Jake Holcomb. They swear by him — and none of them are fools. So — so I believe in Steve too."

She could see that her defense of Steve Cloud angered Ollinger. However, she hardly expected the harshness of the words he now threw at her. "If you do, you're a fool!"

It was Lynn's turn to know anger. She came to her feet, indignant. And while she searched for words to answer this man, she saw, past him in the west, a low-lying amber stain against the sky. Lynn knew what that stain was. Dust. And under a dust cloud that size there had to be many hoofs traveling.

Shining triumph leaped into Lynn's eyes and the flush of eagerness swept her cheeks. "So we'd never see our mules or men we've trusted again, wouldn't we? Take a look at that dust and tell me what's causing it. I know! Mules, and the men who went after them!" She turned and ran, calling the great news to her brother. "Race — Race — ! They're coming. Our mules — !"

Blake Ollinger stared and cursed, and

cursed again. Lynn was right. Dust out there, and under it men and mules.

Down out of the sunset land they came, the dusty mules and the dusty men who brought them. Men haggard and harsh from driving saddle toil and sleeplessness, but men grimly triumphant. And riding with them, humped and fearful and venomous, came Grimes Fallon.

Race and Lynn Ellison ran out to meet them. They stood and watched the strings of mules plod by and Race, noting brands, spoke in some bewilderment. "Those are not the mules we lost, Lynn."

"Does it matter?" cried Lynn softly. "They're mules, which is all that counts." And then her glance reached on to Steve Cloud and drew his eyes to her. She saw the bleak, weary lines in his face soften, saw an answering glow come into his eyes. When he reined in and stepped from his saddle, both her hands went out to him.

"Steve! Oh, it's good to see you back!"

"I hope you never doubted that I'd come back, Lynn?"

"No, Steve — I never doubted. There were times when I was afraid. But that was fear, not doubt."

Race Ellison moved in on Steve. "I see mules all right — Fallon and Overgaard

213

mules. And I see Fallon. What's the story, Steve?"

"A fair trade, Race. Their mules for ours. They stole ours and Fallon agreed to make the trade a good one. I brought Fallon along, just to make sure he didn't change his mind and go back on his word. I can't find it in me to trust the man." There was harsh irony in Steve's last statement.

"I can't imagine Hack Overgaard agreeing to anything like that," said the amazed Race.

"Hack Overgaard is dead," said Steve. "I killed him. He asked for it. He drew first."

As Steve spoke his glance went to Lynn again. Then he sighed deeply, and some of the bitter tautness that had ridden with him ran out of him. For her eyes met his steadily, wide and relieved and without reproach. She said, "I'm sure you did only what you had to do, Steve."

Race Ellison murmured, "I will be damned!" Then a hard grin pulled at his lips. He looked at Grimes Fallon, and he said almost exactly what Steve Cloud had said, back at Calumet: "The trail grows rough, eh, Fallon? And the game works both ways."

Race took over. Brittle orders set the four troublemaking skinners to caring for the mules, watering them, feeding them. Lynn cooked supper, shooing Bueno away when he came to help her.

"You rest, Bueno. I've done nothing but lie around. Now I'm making myself useful."

They ate hugely in the deepening dusk, and immediately after Jake Holcomb sought his blankets. "Time to make up," growled the crusty old skinner. "So we start early tomorrow."

Race Ellison wanted to take Grimes Fallon off their hands, but Pete Orrick spoke up. "If it's all the same to you, Race — me an' Bueno will handle that. We got our reasons."

So, when Pete and Bueno sought their blankets, Grimes Fallon, now tied hand and foot, lay between them. And Bueno said, yawning widely, "I sleep deep but I wake easily. That is to be remembered, Señor Fallon."

"I'll put it plainer," growled Pete Orrick. "You so much as wiggle, Fallon, an' I cool you with a gun barrel. You're goin' all the way to Fort Staley with us — if you're lucky."

Steve was as dead for sleep as the others, but before turning in he had further words with Race Ellison.

"Watch Blake Ollinger, Race — watch

him closely, particularly if he shows signs of doing any unwarranted prowling around. Here's why." Steve went on to tell of the unguarded words Hack Overgaard had blurted out back at the river. "It was an admission that Ollinger was on friendly terms with him and Fallon. I don't know how far that friendship reaches, but it leads straight to the possibility that Ollinger might be in cahoots with them."

Race stared. "Steve, you can't mean that!"

Steve made an irritable gesture. "Damn it, man, of course I mean it. After bumbling out the words Hack Overgaard set out to gun me to close my mouth, obviously because he didn't want the word to reach you. Hell! I'm too tired to make jokes or tell fairy stories."

Race was shaken. His somber glance focused on the dying fire. "Ollinger has given me a lot of damn poor advice. I admit that. Yet it could have been because he never understood the real desert any better than I did. Again, these trail stations of his don't seem to be organized too soundly, but that could be due to the same reason. But to think that he is tied in with Fallon — !" He shook his head. "What do you think he might try to do, Steve?"

"Help Fallon get away from us, for one thing. Or have another try at something he failed to put across back at Station One. Remember that fellow Owens who was found out in front of the ramada with the back of his head knocked in? He was one of Ollinger's men. How did he get killed? Not by an Apache, Race. Bueno killed him. And why? Because he caught Owens sneaking up on me in the night, with a knife in his hand — an Apache knife. The scheme plainly was that I was to be found stabbed to death in my blankets, with an Apache knife. That would have put me out of the way, with the blame going where it didn't belong. But Bueno happened to be on watch and got there first. Damned good and faithful man, Bueno."

"Good God!" breathed Race. "This knocks all the props out from under me. You're saying that the fellow Owens tried to kill you — at Ollinger's order."

"He certainly wasn't trying it for any reason of his own," said Steve curtly. "Owens didn't know me, had never spoken to me or laid eyes on me until we pulled into Station One. He was Ollinger's man. Can you think of a better answer?"

Race was silent. Steve dropped a hand on his arm. "I know it's tough to believe of a man you've figured your friend. But the facts and the logic are straight, Race. Bueno has a word for Ollinger. *Malo* — bad! And Bueno has an instinct in such things. On top of that, I know Ollinger hates me. Remember, this is the desert, and the stakes are high in more ways than one. And I've found that it is safer to judge a man by his acts than by his words. A lot of Ollinger's acts have been damned peculiar."

Race's head came up and around and his eyes met Steve's steadily for a long moment. Then he nodded. "You've been right all the time before, Steve. So I won't argue with you. I'll watch Ollinger."

"Good man! You take over for just this one more night and then we'll work out the future together. Now me for sleep!"

Race was as good as his word. He slept not a wink that night. He listened and he prowled and he watched. He checked his guards carefully and regularly. And he did a lot of very sober thinking.

He went back to the very start of things, checking over in his mind the acts and words of all men with blunt clarity and honesty, and it was as Steve Cloud had told him — the logic was irrefutable. Not a single suggestion Blake Ollinger had given him had turned out sound. The man was either colossally ignorant of the desert and its ways, or he had been deliberately misleading.

Also, he and Ollinger had had words over several angles and the deeper they got into the desert the less willingness to cooperate had Ollinger shown and the more a certain sullenness began to appear. It had been, Race realized, as much Ollinger's persuasion as it had been his own decision to remove Steve Cloud from the job as wagon boss and replace him with Maslin. Which had been a very bad mistake, for after Maslin took over nothing had gone right.

Race found that once he got his thoughts into the channel of doubt the more damning the tide became. Yes, in his acts and advice Steve Cloud had yet to be proven wrong in any of them, while Blake Ollinger was yet to be proven right in any of his.

Race considered the staring stars, the vast night, the down-pressing silence of the desert, and a grimness stole in and settled all through him. This freighting venture of his had been an exciting dream, and he'd been a fool to think it could ever have been put across easily. Nothing was easy in the desert; it was a battle all the way — a battle against time and distance, against heat and hardship, against men and their ways and the ever-increasing danger of the greatest obstacle of all — the Apache!

It was, he realized harshly, high time to sort out all the facts and recognize them clearly. That he proposed to do.

The night seemed a very short one to Steve Cloud. His sleep had been the deep, motionless kind given to a man weary to his very core. But it was also the kind of sleep which fully replenished the wells of a man's strength and vigor, and when Steve awoke to the bustle of a stirring camp, he swung his face to the still-bright stars with the clearest sense of well-being he had known since the start of this desert trip.

For one thing, it seemed that at last all uncertainties had been cleared up, all doubts settled. Race Ellison had toughened up to the desert's hard demands and realities. The threat of interference and trouble from Hack Overgaard and Grimes Fallon had come and been coppered successfully. Blake Ollinger's devious hand had been, if not fully exposed, at least alerted to. There were still many tough miles ahead, plus the growing Apache threat, but at least the trail had at last straightened out and men knew the manner of those they were with and what it was all about. Yeah, things were looking up.

There was some small confusion, getting strange mules lined into teams, but they were off to a start which satisfied even harsh, salty old Jake Holcomb. Jake had one short and profane session with four formerly recalcitrant skinners who had been the source of much trouble. Jake did all the talking, and he found the skinners meek and lacking in retort.

To Race Ellison, just before climbing to the box of his own lead wagon, Jake Holcomb growled, "Jenkins and the other three have sure been civilized. Something tells me we got a tight train now, and a tough one. We'll get along."

They rolled the long, hot day out, with Steve Cloud scouting ahead and laying out the trail. Steve deliberately left the trail to Ollinger's Number Four station, swinging to the south of it.

"The trail Ollinger has picked out leads too close to those humpbacked hills," Steve told Race Ellison. "And there isn't a thing he can offer us at his stations we can't find for ourselves in much safer territory. I know where I'm going, for I scouted this country after I left the train before. There'll be good water for our camp tonight."

Satisfied that all was well ahead, in the middle of the afternoon Steve dropped back

221

to a short distance ahead of the wagons and Lynn Ellison moved out to ride beside him. Steve studied her guardedly then said, "I was wrong, and I apologize."

She colored swiftly. "In what way and why?"

"I didn't think you could stand up to it. The desert and the hardship, I mean." He grinned and added, "You're getting to be a regular old dust-eater."

Her answering laugh was light. "How can anyone help but eat dust when there is so much of it? I find myself wondering at times if there are any places in this part of the world where there isn't any dust."

"Plenty of 'em," vowed Steve. He pointed a long arm. "See that higher country way up north and west of the humpbacked hills? Looks black, doesn't it? Well, that's the distance. When you get closer that black turns to a sort of blue green. Piñon country. I was up there, looking around. You'd never believe it could be so different than the country down here. Sweet, cold water up there, plenty of it. And grass in the meadows and the glades. And the feel of the sun is different. It's warm, but it's got a sparkle to it, and the air is fine and crisp and good to breathe. I'm thinking I'd like to have a ranch up there in the piñons and run cattle. Not all this country is hostile and bitter land."

She looked long at the high country, stained dark with timber. Then she brought her clear-eyed glance back to Steve. "You love it, don't you — the desert?"

He nodded slowly. "Yes, I think I do — when there is no other threat than the desert itself. There are things which travel the desert that I do not like. But once the Apache threat is cleared up there is much of this country that will yield many things to the man who understands it."

She shivered slightly. "I never will forget that lone Apache — on our second day out from Calumet. I wonder why there have not been more?"

"There would have been before this if that lone scout had lived to get away and carry the word. There are others of his kind who have been waiting for his return. They won't wait forever. One of these days they'll act."

As he spoke, Steve's glance swung to the line of humpbacked hills in whose furrowed slopes afternoon's first shadows and mists were beginning to form. The girl seemed to understand. "They are up there?"

"Somewhere up there, yes," said Steve.

"And they'll attack us?"

Steve hesitated slightly. "I'll be mightily amazed if they don't."

They rode on in silence for some time. Abruptly Lynn Ellison spoke of something else. "Do you find yourself missing army life very much, Steve?" She was watching him as she spoke and was a little dismayed at the swiftness with which he seemed to retreat within himself. A moment before he had been party to an easy comradeship. Now, suddenly, he was behind a wall of taciturn reticence.

He was silent so long that Lynn felt she had to speak again. "I wasn't trying to inquire into things that are none of my business," she said gravely. "I brought up the matter so I would have the opportunity to tell you that whatever the cause for your leaving the service, I'm quite sure the fault was not yours."

Again he was silent, and she was sure she had in some way offended. His reply, when it finally came, surprised her. "I know you mean that or you wouldn't have said it. And thanks, Lynn. It means a lot to me to have you believe in me without any explanations. I'll say this: You're right. I wasn't at fault. About your first question — no, I don't find myself missing army life."

He paused, as though measuring a set of values in his mind. "At first I thought I was completely washed up, that there wasn't a single thing worth while left for me in life. Now I know different. Even if my name was cleared and I was offered my commission again, I'm not sure I'd accept. Army life is an insidious thing in a way. It can get into your blood so that no other kind of life seems worth while. But it has its drawbacks too. It sets up a code of values that are perfectly legitimate and desirable within its own scope but which can be rather unrealistic when applied to civilian life."

"I think I know what you mean." Lynn nodded. "I doubt if the confirmed army man ever does fully understand the civilian's viewpoint, nor the civilian understand that of the soldier. We're one and the same as people, yet as individuals we're considerably different."

"That," admitted Steve, "is putting it just about right. There are big and tremendous moments in a soldier's life when on active duty, but there is also a great deal of grinding monotony. I'm not sure I'd want to go back and experience the one at the price of the other. I think" — and now he smiled gravely — "I'm on my way to becoming a pretty good civilian. I find I like being on my own, doing what I like to do without waiting for orders or permission."

Silence fell between them again, but now

Lynn rode with a small and musing smile on her face, as though possessed of some secret satisfaction.

They camped as the first tide of a blue, long-running dusk flooded the desert, camped at the water Steve Cloud led them to. It was a good camp. They rolled the wagons into a compact circle and watered the mules and fed them at the racks of wild hay slung to the wagon sides. Guard shifts were drawn up and established and there was no argument or protest. Jenkins and the other shirkers of the past days now moved to their orders with willingness, and Steve Cloud realized that men were much alike, in service or out. In the long run they reacted favorably to the facts of truth and to stern but fair leadership.

Blake Ollinger had not accompanied the train but had remained back at Station Three. And this suited Steve Cloud and Race Ellison perfectly. Grimes Fallon had ridden under the watchful eye of Race and had spoken no single word all day long, seeming to shrink within himself with every passing mile until his narrow, predatory features were drawn into a beaked mask of hate and desperation. Plainly Fallon believed he was making his last ride.

The night passed without incident and

they were up and away at a time which made Jake Holcomb exult. The grizzled teamster's harsh voice ran back along the string of wagons.

"This is somethin' like. Now we're rollin'. Get it through your heads that we're layin' out a trail that'll be used by plenty a hundred years from now. That's something to think about when the goin' gets tough. Stir 'em up!"

It was a long day, but it was the best they'd had since the start at Calumet. And the water Steve Cloud led them to was the most plentiful they'd yet come to, and there was a stretch of sparse grazing where the mules fed for an hour before being brought inside the wagon circle.

Race Ellison was exuberant over the distance covered and over the manner in which the wagon train had shaken down to order and efficient purpose. He brought his exultation to Steve.

"It's almost like an omen. I've a feeling we're over the worst, Steve."

Steve smiled gravely. "I'd like to believe that. I hope you're right, Race, but I've got to reserve judgment."

"I think you're a confirmed pessimist," jeered Race good naturedly.

"Maybe," drawled Steve dryly. "But the

right word could be — realist."

Good and plentiful water and the far progress of the day lifted other spirits than those of Race Ellison. Steve even heard Jenkins swapping rough jest and relaxed laughter with his three former companions in revolt. But his own mood did not respond too well. There was something stirring in him, something which drew his glance again and again to the north, where the hump-backed hills were now lost in darkness. But even though no longer in sight, Steve knew those hills, and what they could hold, were still out there.

He switched the guard detail, putting himself and Jake Holcomb and Bueno and Pete Orrick on the after-midnight watch. His service experience had taught him that the Apache's favorite moment of attack was just when dawn's grayness broke, and he wanted his most dependable men awake at that time.

"Watch yourselves," he cautioned. "No need to get everybody alarmed unless real trouble shows, but there's a feeling loose in me. I'm remembering the men and mules — or what was left of them — that I found at Ollinger's most advanced camp. The Apache isn't too far away."

The night, however, like the previous one,

passed quietly, and they were off to another early start, mules grunting as they leaned into their collars, wagons creaking and rumbling as they took up a ponderous way once more. Steve moved out in a swift and careful scout, well ahead, and then, when the sun came up to erase all shadows of concealment beside the trail, gradually dropped back until the lead wagon was less than a quarter of a mile behind.

Race Ellison came loping up and dropped in beside him. "You may think this is a damn queer thing to say, Steve — all things considered. When you first said we'd swing away from Ollinger's route, I had another of those damn doubts of mine. Now I know you were completely right. Damned if a queer relief hasn't come over me to be shut of Ollinger. While we were around him, nothing went right. Now we're well away, everything is right. Man! I can see where I'm going to owe you more than I can ever pay. I get the shivers just thinking of the trouble I'd been in if Lynn and I hadn't been lucky enough to get hold of you."

Steve smiled briefly. "Nice of you to say that, but don't go overboard so easy. We're not at Fort Staley yet — not by a lot of miles. Anything can happen. You may yet wish you'd never laid eyes on me." Steve swung his head for another glance at the hump-backed hills which now, due to their progress, lay north and west. That glance, sweeping and casual at first, went abruptly narrow and fixed, and Steve seemed to tower in his saddle and lean a little forward as he pulled his horse to a swinging halt.

Race Ellison was laughing and saying, "I still claim you're just being pessimistic, Steve. If the Apache was really going to hit us, he'd have done it before this. Chances are, even if he was here in the first place, he's pulled out of this part of the country, not liking his new neighbors — the United States Cavalry at Fort Staley."

"Think so?" rapped Steve curtly. "Guess again, Race. Take a look at that!"

Race, his mouth dropping open, stared. From the highest point of the humpbacked hills, dim and pale with distance, yet unmistakable in its reality, a filament of smoke climbed against the sky. Even as Steve and Race watched, the column of smoke wavered and broke and then resumed its climb in uneven blobs which carried a certain spacing.

A gusty breath broke from Race. "Apache?" he gulped.

Steve nodded, his face stony.

"Apache!"

18

It was of no use to try to keep the word from the others in the wagon train. Several of them had seen the smoke signal. Riding back to the train, Steve Cloud called for a halt and gathered everyone around him in council. His glance went around the group.

"We're in for it," he said bluntly. "Just when, just where, your guess is as good as mine. Only one thing is sure. We got a fight ahead of us. Which shouldn't surprise us too much, for it was something to be expected, right from the first. I'd say we're lucky it didn't come before, when we weren't as tightly organized as we are now. Our chances? Just as good as we make them."

Jenkins, the former troublemaker, spoke up, and sturdily. "Let 'em come! They'll know they been over the jumps."

"Now then," growled Jake Holcomb, "that's the kind of talk I like to hear. What's the play, Steve?"

"Why, we push on ahead, of course. We'll

231

pick our camp site for tonight on the basis of defense rather than on water and grass. So it may be a dry camp. Remember that every time you're tempted to reach for your canteens. Make the water you have last. Every man be on the watch at all times, day and night. If we handle ourselves right we can fight through. If I hadn't believed that from the first I wouldn't have come along. Now we roll!"

Steve said to Race Ellison, "I'm going to scout again. I may get quite a distance from the wagons. So it's up to you to take the close-in lead. Don't get over half a mile ahead of the wagons. Use your eyes like never before. Remember, this is Apache country. And an Apache can hide where a lizard couldn't. So you watch yourself!"

To Lynn Ellison, Steve's tone gentled. "I'd give a lot to spare you this. There'll be terror such as you've never known before, for the Apache, more than any other of his kind, gives off terror. But he can be whipped, he can be killed — and he will be. You're going to be a stout feller?"

She was a trifle pale, but her smile was genuine and not in any way forced. "Of course, Steve. I'm tougher than you think. It will be you I'll worry about, riding out there alone."

232

Her hand came out, rested on his arm. He closed his own hand over it. Then he stepped into the saddle and rode.

He swung north for several miles, his rifle across his saddle in front of him, and his constantly swinging glance searched the humpbacked hills in the distance and the earth close at hand. He was remembering words a shrewd old civilian scout had one time spoken during an army patrol.

"The Apache never does things by halves," the scout had asserted. "He either leaves you alone or he hits you like a red-hot chunk of hell. He never wastes himself in any silly hooligan tactics like some of the plains tribes did, raisin' a lot of useless dust an' holler. He comes in quiet, an' he fights mean an' wicked an' plumb for keeps. He's a tough monkey, the Apache."

Steve Cloud had these words in mind as he searched for sign. He knew that a single Apache could move about the country leaving little more visible sign than the momentary shadow of a passing buzzard's wing. But there was bound to be sign if any sizable group was on the move. And this was what Steve wanted to find out.

He found out nothing, saw not a trace of sign, nor did any more smoke signals show in the hills, and at midafternoon he rejoined

233

the wagon train, which had kept to plodding out the steady miles. Race Ellison waited anxiously for his report.

Steve told him what he had and had not seen. "We'll probably have a quiet night tonight," he concluded. "But tomorrow night — !" He shrugged.

The humpbacked hills were definitely behind them now. Race twisted in his saddle to look back at them. "If those hills are an Apache hangout, Steve, you'd think they'd hit us when we were closest to them. Easier for them that way."

"Now you're thinking exactly the way the Apache is hoping we'll think," Steve answered. "The shrewdest scout I ever worked with in the Army claimed that the best weapon in the world to use against the Apache was an understanding of how the Apache mind works. And I saw him successfully prove his theory in a dozen skirmishes."

"And how is the Apache mind working now?" asked Race, half-scoffing.

"Surprise is the prize maneuver of the Apache. He'll work tirelessly to achieve it. The Apache, Race, is fast, deadly, and wicked. I've heard old campaigners, who have fought against all of them, swear the Apache is the most deadly fighter of his kind. And he's smart. He never does the obvious. To handle him, you have to fight just as savagely as he does and, in addition, you've got to outguess him. Fail in either of these and he'll hang your scalp."

"What do you think he's planning for us?" persisted Race.

"Surprise, of course, if possible. Like this. The obvious spot for an attack would have been when we were closest to those hills. Quick to get at us, easy to get back to the cover of the hills. Hit, kill, vanish. Sounds just right, doesn't it? Well, the Apache would figure that that is just exactly what we would figure and expect. Therefore we'd be most alert and on guard while closest to the hills. So he doesn't attack there. He lets us go by, all safe and easy. So maybe we'll think we're past the real danger point and we'll grow less wary and alert. The farther we get away from the hills the sounder we'll sleep and the less guarding we'll do. And then, when and where we least expect it, we'll find the Apache at our throats. Surprise, that's it. And the Apache is a past master at achieving it."

Race took another look at the hills. "You sure don't improve a man's peace of mind," he grumbled.

An hour before sundown they struck

water, a few brackish pools along a badly eroded wash. There was enough for the mules and to replenish canteens. But they did not camp here, for it was a poor place for defense. They pushed on another mile and a half before Steve found a place suitable for the night. Here the wagons were forted and the mules tethered safely inside the circle.

Moving about the camp, Steve could sense the inevitable strain and suspense that were beginning to gnaw at everyone. His own feeling of certainty that an attack was not too far away deepened steadily. It was something a man felt at the back of his neck — in the pit of his stomach. It kept his nerves tingling and taut and it wearied him. Fires were killed immediately the evening meal was eaten, and some men slept fitfully, while others watched and listened and probed the night with grim intentness.

Like the night before Steve would take over a guard post at midnight, and now he was making a final inspection before turning in. A slim shadow moved out of the gloom and fell into step beside him. It was Lynn Ellison. She said not a word, but slim fingers crept into his hand and rested there. It was an instinctive, little-girl action, seeking the comfort of security. And so, silent and hand in hand, they completed the circle of the camp. When this was done and they paused, Steve lifted her hand and cradled it in both of his.

"I'm pretty sure we'll have a quiet night, Lynn," he said softly. "So sleep sound and don't worry."

"If I worry," she replied stanchly, "it will be for Race and you and the others. Never for myself. Good night, Steve."

At his own blankets Steve was pulling off his boots when Bueno drifted up, soft-footed as a cat. "Fallon," murmured the faithful Mexican. "He would speak with you, Señor Steve."

Steve considered, grunted, donned his boots, and went with Bueno to where, as they'd done from the first, Bueno and Pete Orrick had Grimes Fallon between them.

"What is it, Fallon?" rapped Steve curtly.

"You're lookin' for an Apache attack at any time, Cloud. If one comes, where does that leave me? I mean, what chance have I got an' what good can I do without a gun? I don't know what you intend for me, but whatever it is it can't be half as bad as having an Apache tearin' out my throat. I'm demandin' the right to protect myself."

Steve considered for a moment in silence, weighing all factors. Fallon had a certain right in this demand. And Steve well knew that in a close, savage fight one extra man and one extra gun might very well prove the difference between victory or defeat, living or dying. But how could a man put any trust in such as Grimes Fallon?

From the depths of his blankets Pete Orrick growled, "I'd say we were doin' all right just as we are, boy. Don't trust this jigger. He's slippery."

Fallon's voice ran a little shrill. "Damn it, man, all I'm askin' is a chance to defend myself! You'd give that to a dog."

"You can trust a dog," was Pete's acid retort.

Steve cleared his throat. "There'll be a gun for you, Fallon, when and if the Apache hits us. Pete — Bueno — you'll see to that. Trouble breaks, you give Fallon a gun. That's an order. And Fallon, you use that gun for one purpose alone — to shoot Apaches. You make one false move and you'll be shot in your tracks. You hear — Pete and Bueno? That's another order."

"*Si,* Señor Steve," said Bueno. "We understand. It shall be that way."

The night ran its length. Steve Cloud slept, then took over a guard post and saw dawn's grayness come up across a still and peaceful world. And wagons lumbered and rolled again.

The humpbacked hills grew increasingly distant to the north and west, almost vague and a little unreal in the mists of morning. Riding along beside the wagons, Steve sensed a letdown in the tension that had held the camp last night. Evidently there was a feeling among the skinners that they'd left the Apache threat behind. And this, mused Steve, was exactly the reaction the Apache would hope for and gamble on. Grimly he concluded he'd change that feeling when camp was set this night.

Steve contemplated no extended scout this day, for it would serve no purpose. Yesterday's scout had told him all he wanted to know. The Apache was not hovering on their flank or rear. The Apache would be well out in front, would have traveled east out of the humpbacked hills, on a course well to the north of the wagons. And somewhere out there they'd be waiting. So Steve took up his place a few hundred yards ahead of the lead wagon and mentally figured out the course to Fort Staley.

East it would be, and north, across a stretch of country that seemed fairly level but which actually climbed slowly and steadily to a long, running crest hazy with distance. Two days more travel to reach that crest, Steve estimated. And once that was topped, another day and a half of rolling would see them at Fort Staley. Well, they had come a long way already, and each turn of the wagon wheels meant that much more progress against the odds of uncertainty and all the angles of opposition which the desert could throw at them.

Hoofs pattered behind him and Steve turned to see Lynn Ellison coming up. Her smile was a trifle uncertain. "If I'm not supposed to be up here, say so and I'll go back. I want to be a good trooper, Steve."

A sudden rush of feeling ran through him as he looked at her. "You're the best of troopers," he told her, some of his feeling showing in his tone. "And I can think of nothing more pleasant than having you ride beside me."

Color washed up her throat and she looked away. After a little silence she said, "I'm beginning to understand what you see in the desert, Steve — despite its threat. There's a beauty in it, once you've learned how to look for it. Its heat can be like a purifying fire, burning all the dross away. And there is a freedom in it that makes one's thoughts soar. At dawn and dusk and at night is when the beauty blooms. It's a very old land, isn't it? Last night, in my blankets, I tried to understand just how old, and it was a problem beyond me. I fell asleep feeling very small and useless and of no consequence at all. Does that sound silly?"

"If it is," declared Steve, "then I've known a lot of the same, for I've often thought such things myself. A man has to be much around the things he has built to feel outsize. I remember a high-ranking officer fresh out from the East on an inspection trip —" He broke off, as if this delving into the past had stirred up unpleasant recollections.

Lynn looked at him. "Please go on."

He surprised her by laughing, a low laugh, rich with a near-forgotten humor. It was the first real laugh she'd yet heard from him.

"He was a tremendous fellow — in his own estimation," said Steve, his laugh running into a reminiscent chuckle. "He knew the book by heart. But the desert had never heard of the book. It fried and roasted and sweated him. It covered his buttons with dust and soaked his best tailored breeches with horse sweat. A hundred miles in the saddle was a lot different than a few hours a day in a swivel chair. He was scalded and peeled, and a minor fracas with the Apache stood his hair on end. The inspection trip was cut short and he left for the East again in a hurry, swearing that the desert was an outpost of hell and not worth fighting for, which he would so recommend to the proper authorities."

Now Lynn laughed with Steve. "Oh, you put it so perfectly. I can just see him, Steve. I'll bet he was a rather stout man and just full of pompous snorts and stern throat clearings."

"Exactly!" Steve grinned. "At first — but not when he left. Then he was the most disillusioned individual you ever saw. In a way, the post hated to see him go. Everybody enjoyed the experience except the man himself. Colonel Toyenbee himself remarked privately that it was one of the best shows he'd ever seen."

They talked of many things as they rode the miles down — things that had no relation to the desert or the threat it held at all. For they were young, and youth's thoughts are elastic and eager. There was cunning in the way Lynn drew him out, broke down the armor of reticence he'd carried so long. And she secretly rejoiced in what she saw beyond that armor. A man who was thrusting a bitter past far into the background and mists of forgetfulness and facing the future with new eagerness and optimism.

On his part, Steve was increasingly aware of this girl beside him, of the fine, feminine charm of her. The desert, as he well knew from experience, had a way of bringing out the best or the worst in a person. In this girl it had found courage and spirit and a fine sweetness which neither hardship nor danger could dilute. He liked the quick alertness of her mind and the breadth of her thoughts. A man of education himself, he had on many past occasions hungered for an intelligence to match his own. In Lynn Ellison he found it.

Race Ellison came up and joined them, and the fine moment was broken, for Race was full of the practical facts of the day. He pointed to that dim crest far ahead.

"Tough pull up to there, Steve, but I've a feeling it's a dividing line of some sort. We cross it and we've left the worst behind. It'll be a great moment when I first see Fort Staley out past my horse's ears."

Steve shrugged, his tone going dry. "Never try to anticipate in the desert, Race. Accept the best moments only when they've actually arrived. That way you'll never be disappointed."

Race stirred impatiently in his saddle. "Man, when are you going to quit doubting and admit we're there?"

"When we actually are. Time enough then to whoop and cheer."

There was water under that long slope

243

and it came to the surface almost in the center of a wide, saucer-flat basin. There were several miles of sunshine left when the wagons creaked into the basin, but Steve called for the camp at this spot. He had a long look all around, then nodded as though he had readied some kind of conclusion.

Watching him, Race asked, "What does that mean? You've decided on something."

"I think it will be tonight or not at all," said Steve. "As the desert goes, we're not so awfully far from Fort Staley. The Apache knows where we're heading and he's smart enough to realize that in Fort Staley they are waiting for these supplies. Which brings up a reasonable probability that there could be a troop of cavalry heading out this way to meet us. I'm not saying there is, so don't get your hopes up. But there could be. If that troop should show and join up with us, the Apache's hope for a raid is gone. So he'll strike before the possibility becomes fact."

Steve swung his arm and went on. "The Apache likes to hit from above. As far as this wagon train is concerned, here is his first opportunity to do so. This is going to be a long night, Race. I've a feeling about it."

Steve saw to it that the wagons were forted with extra care, in a tight circle about the water hole. There was a little graze in the basin, and the mules were allowed to make the most of this while daylight lasted. Then they were brought inside the circle and tethered strongly. Jake Holcomb saw to that.

"A mule with an arrow in it and breaking loose inside a wagon circle can raise hell," growled the old fellow. "Set those knots up extra strong."

Supper was eaten before daylight faded completely, and fires were quenched. And as soon as full dark had fallen Steve set men to work with buckets, scooping water from the water hole and splashing it all across the wagon canvas. The sun-parched stuff sucked up the moisture greedily and grew damp and dark.

"Fire arrows can be bad," Steve explained. "Nothing the Apache likes to see more than a wagon burning. It sets mules crazy and it gives the Apache light to see more targets. But this canvas won't burn."

In posting his guards, Steve was guided more by the problem of defense than the consideration of mere watchfulness. For once the Apache struck he would come in fast and close — he would do his utmost to carry a charge through. It was his way.

The upper half of the basin would be the point of greatest danger and that side of the wagon circle would take the heaviest impact, so Steve placed his men accordingly. There would be no split guard shift tonight, he explained. It would be continuous duty for everyone all night long. Low barricades of gear were thrown up for men to fight behind, weapons made ready, plenty of ammunition laid out. Then came the wearing wait through the long, dark hours.

At regular intervals Steve made his rounds, stopping to hold low-voiced talk with each man. He dropped down beside Jenkins, past troublemaker. "How's everything?" he murmured.

"Good enough," Jenkins answered. "Man gets queer feelin's at a time like this. You look for somethin' long enough you think you see it. You're ready to swear there's somethin' out there. Then you close your eyes quick and tight, an' when you open them again for another look, you know damn well you ain't seen a thing."

Steve laughed softly. "Know exactly what you mean. First patrol I ever went on I shot all hell out of a chunk of choya cactus, ready to swear it was an Apache coming in with a knife two feet long. As it happened, there wasn't a hostile within fifty miles of that camp. Did I take a going over from the senior in command! Man alive! I'll bet there never was, before or since, a rookie lieutenant who was scraped to the raw like I was."

He heard Jenkins' answering chuckle. "We all have to learn a lesson, I reckon. I've learned mine."

Steve dropped his hand on the man's shoulder. "No hard feelings then, Jenkins?"

"Hell — no! Why should there be? I had it comin'. I was a damn fool. I'll be skinnin' an outfit for Race Ellison as long as he'll have me."

"Good man!" said Steve, moving on.

Steve came up with Pete Orrick. "Where's Fallon, Pete?"

"Yonder — tied to a wagon wheel."

Steve went over, dropped on his heels beside the prisoner. "Readjusted your ideas any, Fallon?"

"You're a fool to keep me tied up this way," snapped Fallon. "What the devil! Give me credit for havin' some sense, Cloud. Would I be stupid enough to try to sneak out on you now? Hardly! Put myself alone and afoot out in country probably crawlin' with Apaches? I wouldn't be doin' you any particular harm, if that's what I was still after, while I'd be askin' to have the Apache stake me out on an anthill. Get these ropes off me an' give me a gun. You can use me. "

Steve considered in silence. The man's argument made sense. Steve began untying knots. "All right — I'll do it. I don't suppose you'd care to say anything about Blake Ollinger?"

Fallon knew what he meant. "Not now. Later we'll see. If we're still alive."

He rubbed his wrists where the ropes had been. Steve got him a Sharps rifle and a bag of ammunition and posted him at a guard spot. Fallon got close to the earth with a grunt of satisfaction. "I'll be on hand an' useful when the fun starts, Cloud."

Moving along, Steve found Bueno beside him. The squat, faithful Mexican was like a cat in the dark. Bueno swung a hand that took in the upper slope of the basin. "I would go out there, Señor Steve. It would help to know that they were really there."

"Not at the price of a knife in your back, Bueno."

The Mexican's laugh was soft. "That would not be easy to do, señor — even for an Apache. Have no worries."

"All right," agreed Steve. "You're right — it would help. But not too far, Bueno. At the first sign you must get back here. That's a promise?"

"A promise, señor." Bueno vanished, silent as a shadow.

Race Ellison was at his guard post, his

sister curled up beside him. Steve Cloud hunkered down on his heels. "Bueno is making a little scout," he remarked.

"No need," said Race. "They're out there."

"How do you know?" A note of amusement was in Steve's voice, put there deliberately for Lynn's sake. "You haven't seen anything?"

"No. And I can't smell 'em, either. But the hair on the back of my neck won't smooth down. Damnedest feeling I ever had in my life, but it tells me things."

Lynn's soft shoulder pressed against Steve and she was trembling slightly. "You told me there'd be terror, Steve. Now I know what you meant." Her voice was little more than a whisper.

Steve put an arm around her and she did not draw away. Presently her trembling stopped and she went completely still and relaxed, like a comforted child.

Steve was content to remain just so while the night deepened and seemed to take on a deep, slow breathing as though in slumber. Lynn's head fell back against his arm, then rolled until it was against his shoulder. Abruptly he realized that this girl was sleeping too.

Her hair brushed his cheek when he turned his head. It smelled of sunshine.

Some time later he let her gently down against the earth, got a blanket, and covered her. To Race he murmured, "If an attack does come, we'll need every gun, Race. But your main job is to take care of Lynn. That's understood?"

"Of course. What time is it?"

Steve looked at the stars. "Just short of midnight. Considerable wait yet."

Bueno reappeared, and Steve gripped the Mexican's arm in relief. "This is our fight, señor," reported Bueno. "The Apache is out there."

In a way the words were a relief, thought Steve. Nothing chewed up a man as badly as uncertainty. Waiting was bad enough, but when you combined uncertainty with it, then it really worked on a man's nerves. But when you knew, even though the knowing meant sure promise of deadly combat, then you felt better because you could definitely set yourself for what was ahead.

Steve made the rounds again, relaying Bueno's information. Men quickened to a new alertness. Grimes Fallon was where Steve had left him and took the news with a noncommittal grunt. Then he said, "I been thinkin', Cloud. I could stop a slug or an arrow. So I better do my talkin' now. About Ollinger. He was in this deal with Overgaard an' me from the very start. It was our money he used to put up those trail stations. The idea was to get Ellison way out in the desert an' then rig things so he'd be stranded an' sick of the whole deal. Then we'd buy him up through Ollinger. We needed somebody who passed as a friend in Ellison's camp, an' that was Ollinger. It was a good deal an' would have worked — except for you."

Steve considered in silence. Then he said, "Feel better to get it off your chest, Fallon?"

"Yeah. But not for the reason you think. Not because I like you any better, or because I'm gettin' religion now the chips are down. But because I never did really trust Blake Ollinger, even though he was workin' with Overgaard an' me. I always had the feelin' he would double-cross us as well as Ellison, if he could. A really honest man stands on his own worth, Cloud — an' I can even understand an' in some way respect an honest crook, if you get what I mean? But a crooked crook like Ollinger — hell with him!" Fallon spat.

"You make your distinctions pretty clear," said Steve dryly. "Well, we're in for it. Good luck!"

Men — and their ways! Steve mused on this as he circled on. They lived as they did for reasons of their own and to codes of conduct that satisfied them. Some were perverted codes and others were clear and open. Even the crooked ones had their own philosophies, sometimes never given openly, but at other times spoken, as Grimes Fallon had spoken just now.

When you tried to figure it out you ended up nowhere, for what made sense to one did not add up for another. And the reality and pressure of events forced their conduct. You never knew exactly where you'd find courage or cowardice. Maybe it all depended on what value a man placed on his own life. Human nature — the greatest riddle of them all. . . .

Time swung its remorseless course. With Bueno helping him, Steve carried more water and sluiced the wagon tops again. Fire, more than any one thing, could break up the tight security of the forted wagons. If, thought Steve grimly, the Apache was banking on surprise, this was one to throw back at him.

The feel of the night changed. The small cold hours came and went. Almost imperceptibly the sky to the east paled. The subdued cry of a night bird echoed thinly across the upper slope of the basin. Bueno hissed his alarm.

"Señor Steve — they come — !"

11

It was Jenkins who fired the first shot. Something that he'd been seeing in fancy all the long night through finally became reality. A low-crouched, swiftly scudding thing that was only the dimmest of shadows against dawn's first thin light. But real this time — very real!

The hoarse roar of the big Sharps rifle rocked the stillness, bounced its echoes across the slope. And Jenkins had fired shrewdly, holding low against the false dawn's deceit. That scudding shape spun around and melted into earth's blackness. And then outside the wagon circle all the slope seemed alive.

That first rush carried almost up to the wagons. Had there been the slightest laxity in guarding, the rush would have carried home to a deadly, bloody finality. But now the rush was met by the pounding fury of those heavy rifles, and the charge wavered and broke and melted back, and there was a full dozen bullet-torn warriors to mark the forward limit of the savage tide.

Steve Cloud, lying close to earth under a wagon, so that he might catch lithe, darting figures against the swiftly paling stars, had loaded and fired, loaded and fired, knowing that he missed some, knowing that he hit others. One racing figure, with loose ends of a calico headband streaming behind, might have been a winged, malignant mercury, until a smashing slug from Steve's rifle took him, knocking him end over end. Those big Sharps slugs were murderous.

The tide ebbed, but returned, this time in a manner Steve had luckily anticipated. The night seemed full of the flutter and hiss of curving arrows. Some of these arrows flamed, curving up and out and down across the sky. They struck canvas wagon tops and stuck there, burning. Wet canvas smoldered but did not flame. The arrows flickered out.

More of the same came, but with no better luck. Fire would not be a scorching ally of the Apache this time. Yet one such soaring torch, sailing clear across the circle of the wagons, landed in a feed rack on a wagon side, where a small bunch of wild hay still rested. The hay began to flame. It was Bueno who dipped up a bucket of water, raced to the spot, and sluiced out the danger.

But the Apache was smart. He'd always been smart. He knew the make-up of mules. He began curving his arrows higher, to clear the wagons and drop among the tethered mules. A flaming arrow dug into a mule's flank, clung there, and the animal went mad. Here was what Jake Holcomb had feared. The harsh old skinner darted in and shot the mule through the head just as it tore loose from its tether in a wild, crazy lunge. And then an arrow that did not flame, but came whistling in on invisible wings, ripped across Holcomb's ribs, the shock of it spinning him half around. Holcomb staggered a little as he ran back to his defense post.

The Apache made his second rush. Cat figures in the false light gone berserk with ferocity. Some died, others came on. One dauntless demon lunged between two wagons, sunk a knife to the hilt in a teamster, only to be brained the next instant by Pete Orrick's gun butt.

For several long moments after the attack first struck Grimes Fallon saw nothing to shoot at. Then he glimpsed movement in a stealing circle. He cursed when he missed his first shot, cursed again — but with satisfaction this time — when he killed a warrior on his second try.

There was no well of genuine courage in

Grimes Fallon, but there was a driving desperation to live. And so he fought, as he had promised Steve Cloud he would fight if given the chance. He lay there, glimpsing elusive targets, taking the jarring recoil of the big Sharps, coughing as the acrid powder smoke washed back into his face.

He killed another scudding demon; there was no mistaking the way the heavy bullet knocked the Apache all crooked and winding and limp before the earth took him. He thought he had winged another, and he lifted himself higher for a better look. He took a solidly chunking arrow fairly through the throat. He knew no pain, no agony. He knew nothing at all. . . .

The warrior, dying himself, but tenacious as a mad catamount, came crawling in and made sure of Fallon with a knife thrust before going to his wild fathers.

The second rush faltered and gave back. Steve Cloud, measuring the steadily growing light in the east, lifted a shout.

"Steady — everybody! They may try once more — !"

Lynn Ellison, crouched low beside her brother and knowing now indeed the full measure of the terror Steve Cloud had foreseen, let out a little sob of relief at the sound of Steve's voice.

The third try came and was a wicked one. The Apache knew it was the final chance, for now the false light of day was becoming real. A withered but hawk-faced and implacably hating chieftain sent them in and they took his word and did their best. The hoarse fury of the defending Sharps thundered at them and beat them down, but some still came on.

One of them got through and dived at Steve Cloud behind a glitter of naked and thirsting steel. Steve threw his empty rifle at the warrior and the Apache stumbled over it but came up snarling soundlessly. It took two shots from Steve's heavy six-shooter to put the warrior down. Ah — they were fighters, these Apache!

Pete Orrick, the growing light giving him a chance at his most distant target, shot carefully, and that withered, exhorting chieftain died before the lethal power of the hurtling slug. And somehow the attackers knew, and it marked the finish.

And so it ended as swiftly as it had begun. There were no more fluttering, hissing arrows, no more darting demons. They melted into nothingness, and only their dead which lay closest to the wagons were left for day's real light to disclose.

Men drained by battle fury, blackened

with powder stain, waited while the light spread and dawn's grayness became shot with pearl and rose, and when the first spear of sunlight lanced across the world they stared and blessed it.

There was no exultation, there was only weariness and the curious, mechanical numbness that were the aftermath of battle. Steve Cloud's first thought was Lynn Ellison. When he saw her standing safe within the circle of her brother's arm he stumbled up to them, and his voice was a dry croak.

"This makes it worth while." Then he added, somewhat inanely, "It'll be a late start this morning."

They took stock of casualties. Two were dead — Grimes Fallon and one of the former troublemaking teamsters, Plank. Jake Holcomb had an arrow gouge across his ribs and Pete Orrick had a stain of dried blood at the angle of his jaw where just the faintest kiss of an arrow had touched. One mule was dead — the one Jake Holcomb had had to shoot, two others had minor arrow wounds.

"I don't know why our luck was so good," said Steve Cloud.

"I do," growled Jake Holcomb, chewing tobacco furiously against the pain of having

258

his wound cleaned and bandaged. "It was your savvy in havin' the wagon tarps wet down — that an' havin' every man on his toes an' ready when they hit. But them wet wagon tarps was the real ace in the hole. The 'Pache figgered to get the wagons to burnin'. Had he been able to we'd have knowed we'd really been to a waltz. But when the tarps wouldn't ketch, then all the 'Pache could do was hit straight out an' we were ready for that."

Steve took another look at the sun. "We've things to do, but we'll roll again in an hour. I don't think there'll be any more trouble ahead but country and distance."

In his quarters at Fort Staley, Major Dan Blair gulped a glass of lukewarm water and soundly cursed the heat, bumbling fate, and the dark iniquity which lay deep in the souls of some men. He looked across the hot half-gloom of the room at his daughter, who stood at the window, staring pensively out at the sweltering rectangle of reddish-brown earth that was the parade ground. Despite his inner feelings, the major kept his tone gentle.

"We've got to square things for Steve Cloud, Hetty."

Hetty Blair Matlock nodded. "Yes — we must do that."

"If we only knew where to locate the boy," said the major. "He left upriver from Yuma, according to Jason Toyenbee's advices. Lord knows where he is now." The major poured another glass of water, swallowed it without relish.

He was a man of average size, slender, very straight of spine, a bit on the dapper side, but a proven soldier. He was generous with his men but a martinet with himself, particularly where his physical condition was concerned. He was trim and lean and brown, and despite the generous salting of gray in his close-trimmed brown hair, looked a good ten years younger than his sixty years.

"If only that trooper Dagland had had his falling out with Matlock before the court-martial," grumbled the major.

"Yes," agreed the girl quietly. "And before I married Ellis Matlock. But let's not blame others, Father. Let's blame ourselves. For being blind and stupid and — and unfair." Just the faintest quaver touched her last words.

The father eyed his daughter in commiseration. "You've definitely made up your mind — about Matlock?"

Her nod was quick, sure. "Quite definitely. I'm leaving him. I simply could not go on living in the same house with a man for whom I've lost every last shred of respect. He's resigning the service, of course?"

The major cleared his throat a little harshly. "The Army is allowing him to do that. More generosity than he deserves. Child, I'm awfully sorry about all this."

"Don't be," she said quickly. "Not for me. I want no one to be sorry for me. The mistake was my own. I alone am to blame."

The major's eyes softened. This daughter of his had courage. "Proud of you, youngster," he said simply.

An orderly knocked at the door, entered to the major's summons. "Sergeant Daley's compliments, sir. That wagon train of supplies we've been expecting has just arrived. And, sir — Lieutenant — or — Mister Stephen Cloud is with it."

"The devil!" Major Blair's head jerked up. "Thank you, Connors. Tell Sergeant Daley I'll be right out."

The orderly hurried away. Major Blair took his hat off the table, his eyes on his daughter. She had stiffened at the orderly's words and stepped back a little from the window.

"I should invite the boy in, daughter," said the major.

"Of course. We must be very fair and honorable about everything, Father." There were no tears in her eyes, but there were in her voice.

The major sighed and went out.

At first sight of Fort Staley, Steve Cloud had known a quick and stabbing stirring within him. Though the setting might be different there was a certain similarity to all these southwest frontier military posts, for all held like components. Fort Staley was built later than any of the others Steve had known, but already the sun was toning down that newness, bleaching and beating out its own pattern.

The old things, the half-forgotten things that had been so much a part of his life — the flag, drooping at its halyards in the hot, motionless air. The leathery, sun-blackened faces of men in uniform; the regulated procedure and manner of greeting. The feel of the layout, invisible but always there. The ammoniac smell of stables and corrals baking in the sun. . . .

That erect, almost dapper figure, angling across now from the officer's row! Steve had to look twice to be sure. Then Steve stepped from his saddle, stood silent, hiding his surprise behind a mask of taciturnity.

Major Dan Blair put out his hand. "Stephen — a pleasure. Greater than you can imagine. You haven't heard?"

Steve shook his head, bewildered. What was the meaning behind that eagerly outstretched hand? "I've heard nothing, sir. What — ?"

"We'll go into that later, in my quarters. This is your wagon train?"

Steve shook his head again. "No. I'm merely wagon boss and guide, perhaps. Race and Lynn Ellison are the owners. They hold the freighting contract. Come meet them."

Race and Lynn stood by the lead wagon. "Major Blair," announced Steve quietly. "Major, meet Race Ellison and Miss Lynn Ellison."

The major was very cordial. "My pleasure," he said, bowing over Lynn's hand. "While you are here you will accept the hospitality of the post. We are happy to extend what comforts we have. You will be the guests of my daughter and myself at dinner tonight."

Lynn saw Steve Cloud stiffen, saw his face darken and turn grim. "Lynn and Race will be glad to accept, Major. For myself — I'll be busy. My thanks and regrets to you and — Mrs. Matlock."

The major winced, then said briefly, "Things you do not understand, my boy."

He turned to a burly trooper with a sergeant's stripes. "You will see to all details of unloading, Daley!"

"Yes, sir!"

"We've a wounded teamster with us, Major," said Steve. "A little Apache trouble along the way. The wound is coming along all right, I think, but I'd like the post physician to have a look at it."

"Of course. Daley, you will see to that also." The major took Steve by the arm. "You and I must have a talk immediately. I insist upon that. Connors, you will escort Mr. Ellison and Miss Ellison to my quarters and make proper introductions to Mrs. Matlock."

Connors, the orderly, saluted.

The major's grip on Steve's arm steered him across the corner of the parade ground to the orderly room. It was hot in there and a company clerk with a red and sweating face came to attention as the major entered.

"You may seek a cooler place for a while, Jensen," said the major by way of dismissal.

The moment they were alone Major Blair faced Steve directly. "The Army is offering you your commission back again, my boy."

Steve stood silent, meeting the major's eyes. Then he said, "I don't understand."

"The findings at your court-martial have

turned out to be in gross error," the major told him. "Deep injustice was done to you. That is to be rectified. We'll be happy to have you back with us."

Steve's expression did not change. "I still don't understand, sir."

The major squirmed. "Evidence has turned up that the fault was that of Captain Matlock, who was senior in command at the time. Captain Matlock's claims and testimony have been proven false. In other words" — and here the major's formality of word and manner left him entirely — "Matlock has turned out to be a damned liar and a scoundrel and is being far more fairly treated than he deserves by being allowed to resign the service. A certain trooper, by name of Dagland, has been dishonorably discharged for the good of the service. Another scoundrel, Stephen, who accepted money and favor from Matlock for giving false testimony at your court-martial. It appears that the promised money and favor were not entirely forthcoming. Matlock and Dagland quarreled about that and Dagland, with just enough sutler's whisky in him to grow careless, blurted out the whole story. New investigation proved that this time Dagland was telling the truth. Your name and record have been cleared, Stephen."

Steve stared past the major at the barren wall of the orderly room, not seeing it. Abruptly he turned and walked out. The major understood, stood watching the empty door for a moment. Then he sighed, mopped sweat from his face, left the place himself, and headed for his quarters.

The major's dinner that night was hardly a success, though Steve Cloud, reversing his original decision, attended it. Steve had shaved and scrubbed up but wore the only clothes he possessed, the worn, stained ones of the long trail. Race Ellison was in the same predicament, but Lynn, with true feminine resourcefulness, came up in a dress that looked crisp and cool and gave to her a sort of serene loveliness which startled Steve and held him thoughtful.

His one tough moment came when he faced Hetty Blair Matlock. He wondered what it would do to him, and he knew one of his greatest moments of relief when he realized it did nothing. Nothing at all. Hetty Blair Matlock was just another woman, the prettiness that had once been hers somewhat faded now. She was older, quieter — and hurt. Steve knew only one emotion. He was sorry for her.

The major tried valiantly to make talk. He explained that he was only temporarily in command at Fort Staley. An emergency thing, that had transferred him up from Bowie. As soon as his relief arrived his orders for the future would take him East. Both Hetty and he would be glad to get away from the desert, he said. They'd had enough of it.

Steve did not miss the inference in these words. If Hetty was traveling with her father, it meant that she was done with Ellis Matlock. Well, people were responsible for certain things in their lives — and some of them made mistakes.

"I've only one regret," Major Blair was saying, "and that is not being able to serve in the field again with you, Stephen."

It was the opening Steve had been waiting for. "Then you can lay that regret away also, Major. You see, I'm not going back into service again. Naturally I'm happy over having my name cleared and all that. But I've found I like the life of a civilian. I've plans for the future — for things I'd be unable to do if I accepted a commission again."

The major was frankly startled. The service had been his life for so long he could not conceive of any other being more acceptable. "You're sure you're not making a mistake, my boy?"

"Quite sure."

Steve felt Lynn Ellison's eyes. They were glowing. He did not try to meet those of Hetty Blair Matlock, for he knew they'd be tired and disillusioned and a little old. . . .

The wagons rolled on the back trail two days later. Men and mules were full fed, full rested. Major Blair, inquiring more fully into the Apache trouble they'd had on the trip in, suggested an escort part of the way. Steve Cloud shook his head.

"Entirely unnecessary, Major — but thanks just the same. We punished them savagely in the attack. I'd say a couple of patrols sent through those humpbacked hills would clear them out completely. In any event, we're not worried. We're a pretty tight outfit and know our way around by this time. Good luck, sir —. to you and — to Hetty."

So they shook hands, and that was that. And Steve Cloud did not look back when he rode away.

12

The miles seemed shorter on the way back to Calumet and the river. For the trail was set now. They knew the distances and they knew about water, and the empty wagons rolled easily. They forted the wagons at night and they put out guards. They passed the scene of the attack and they watched the humpbacked hills move in and drop behind them, and there were no smoke signals or sign of hostiles anywhere.

The awareness came to them that perhaps their biggest difficulties were all behind them. They had established the route and had beaten the wild country in itself. If the Apache struck again they knew what to expect, what to do. And they would not be afraid. The desert had tried them, seasoned them, had not found them wanting, and so accepted them.

Steve Cloud rode a scout to the north, touched Blake Ollinger's Number Four trail station, found it deserted. No death was here, but neither was there life. The ramada and the corrals stood empty and deserted. At camp that night he reported his findings to Race Ellison. Race shrugged.

"If we needed further proof about Ollinger, I guess that is it. He had nothing behind him but Overgaard and Fallon. Now they're gone so — !" Race shrugged again.

"Fallon did all right at the finish," Steve said.

"Yeah, he did." Race nodded. "But by choice or necessity? I don't believe the man ever stopped hating."

Steve had no good answer to that. You never knew, he decided, all about any man. You might guess, but you could never be sure. Not a man like Fallon, anyway.

Steve had his first moment alone with Jenkins since the attack. "I'm mighty sorry about Plank. He was your friend."

"Yours, too, at the end," replied Jenkins quietly. "He told me so. He knew that you'd been right all along, just the same as I did. We were the ones who'd been wrong. Well, he died with the satisfaction of knowing he'd proved up when it counted. No man can ask a better finish."

Steve marveled a little at the change in Lynn Ellison. The real hardships of the trail seemed to have no effect on her whatever. She was bright and gay and cheery and seemed full of a new eagerness for life. Steve found a steadily deepening contentment just in her presence. One evening when they found themselves alone beside the campfire she shot a sudden question at Steve.

"No regrets?"

Steve looked at her. "Regrets about — what?"

"Turning down the offer of a return of your commission."

Steve's words held a firm definiteness. "Not a regret." He went silent for a moment while he loaded and lit his pipe. "I didn't turn down the offer because of any lingering bitterness or sense of injustice. I left all that behind me long ago. What I told Major Blair was the truth. I like this life better. I never dreamed I would, but I do."

"I'll always be curious about the original trouble, Stephen."

Steve smiled faintly. "I've been waiting the chance to give you the story. There wasn't a great deal to it. There was a patrol sent out to guard a wagon train. Captain Ellis Matlock was in command of the patrol. An ambitious man, Matlock, hungry for promotion, too ambitious to follow the rules of ordinary caution.

"We knew where we were supposed to meet up with the wagon train. Miles before we reached this spot Matlock ordered me to take part of the patrol and ride a scout in a side direction, to ride as far as a certain hill point and look for Apache sign. After doing that I was to rejoin the main patrol and the wagon train. It was a verbal order, delivered in front of Matlock's orderly, a trooper named Dagland. Because the order did not make sense to me, I asked Matlock to repeat it. He did so, with emphasis. I still argued with him, for it was bad Apache country and splitting the patrol, which was small enough to begin with, was dangerous procedure as I saw it. I tried to point this out to Matlock. He would not listen to me, being the sort who felt that to reverse an order was a sign of weakness and poor military judgment. So there was nothing left to me but obey."

Steve touched a freshening match to his pipe. "I led my part of the patrol to the designated point of hills. We found Apache sign, all right — too much. And heading in a direction I did not like. We rode fast then, to contact the rest of the patrol and the wagon train. It was over when we got there. The Apache had struck in force and with surprise. The wagon train was wiped out — burned. Matlock and his part of the patrol had been roughly handled, badly shot up, and the survivors forced to retreat in a hurry."

Lynn was listening with breathless intensity. She saw the memory of several dark days drag a grimness across Steve Cloud's face.

"Matlock knew that he would be held to account for splitting his patrol and he was. That was when the lying started." A thread of bitterness crept into Steve's voice. "When Colonel Crittenden, in command of Fort Bowie at the time, went after Matlock for splitting his patrol, Matlock swore I'd gone beyond my direct orders, that I'd been ordered out but a few miles on the flank to scout, which was sound enough military strategy. Matlock claimed I'd been ordered not to get beyond immediate touch with the main patrol. And Dagland, the only other man to hear the original order, swore that this was so. There was left only my word against both of theirs, and one of them was my senior in command. So the blame was shifted from Matlock to me and the court-martial was ordered."

"How contemptible and unfair!" blazed Lynn. "How could the court-martial board have believed them and not you?"

Steve smiled faintly. "Sometimes a man can be the biggest kind of chivalrous fool. I was. I didn't offer too much defense."

"But — why? Why should any man accept the blame for another's mistake? Why should he — Oh! I know!" Lynn came to her feet. "You did it — for her! For Hetty Blair Matlock! Stephen Cloud, you did!"

Steve nodded slowly. "They were to be married. At one time I thought I was pretty fond of Hetty Blair. I liked her father. The Army and all it represented was their whole life. I — I guess I was pretty mixed up. Anyhow, I played the part of a very noble young fool. As things have turned out, I'm glad I did. I haven't really been hurt a bit."

Lynn went very still. Then she said, "You must have cared an awful lot for her. Maybe you still do. Maybe —"

"No, Lynn. I didn't — and I don't. I just thought I did. But I know better now. You'd have to live the life to fully understand. Duty at one of these frontier army posts is a life within itself. There are the big, strong moments when actual conflict is going on. But between those moments is a monotony that can twist a man's perspective all out of shape. Women are scarce. To an impressionable young officer the plainest, most ordinary woman in the world can seem a creature of enchantment. His eyes become fogged. He sees things that really aren't there at all. But once he gets away from the life, then he realizes the truth. I'm sorry for Hetty Blair — that's all. And I'm sorry for her father. Major Dan Blair is a good man."

Watching him closely, Lynn saw the quiet truth, and relaxed. "This — this Captain Matlock, what about him, Stephen?"

"He and Trooper Dagland quarreled. Dagland, full of sutter's whisky, blurted out the truth. Matlock was allowed to resign the service, probably out of respect for Major Blair and Hetty. Such things have a way of squaring themselves in the long run."

Lynn stared at the fire. She spoke of Hetty Blair. "Poor thing. She'll have a lifetime of regrets."

Steve smiled faintly. Knowing Hetty Blair, he doubted this. Time, another post of duty — new faces — He kept this opinion to himself. Right now it was far more pleasant and interesting to observe the way the fading fire glow picked out highlights on Lynn Ellison's face and softened the clean curve of her throat.

They swung north and picked up Ollinger's Station Three. This also was deserted. But the water was there and they'd use this on future trips.

"I never will like this damn camp," said

Race Ellison. "For here was where we lost our mules and where I thought everything had collapsed around my ears. We had to travel this far to learn our full lesson, eh, Lynn?"

She colored, throwing a swift glance at Steve Cloud. "Knowing all we know now, Race, I marvel we could have been such fools."

West the wagons rolled, and the sun blazed and the dust lifted and the desert dropped more of its immensity behind them. There was a certain cadence to their pace now. Every man knew his chore and did it. All was smooth efficiency. They were a solidly integrated thing now and it was a pleasure to be part of it.

Race Ellison had reason to believe that the next shipment of army supplies to come upriver would be considerably larger than the last. Which would mean more wagons, more mules, more men. The prospect did not worry him. He would have several weeks in which to round up these necessities.

The nights made the days worth while. Coolness letting down from the star-brightened heavens. Beauty of evening shadows and the eagerness of each new dawn. And for Steve Cloud that constantly growing awareness of Lynn Ellison. Even in the desert, thought Steve, there was no lack of life's richest ingredients if a man's eyes were clear and his balance sound.

Blake Ollinger's stations two and one were as empty as the others. It was when they had passed the last of these that Pete Orrick came to Steve Cloud.

"Boy," said Pete bluntly, "what do you make of this Ollinger hombre? Looks like he's pulled stakes and cleared out. But me — I'm wonderin' how far? Bueno an' me, we been talkin' about these things. We see 'em alike. That Ollinger — he's what Bueno claims. *Malo!* Bad! He ain't the kind to forget easy. He'll pack a hate to his dyin' day — for you. Because it was you who busted his fine little scheme all to hell an' gone. He ain't goin' to forget that — an' don't you forget it. Me an' Bueno, we're goin' to keep our eyes open when we hit Calumet an' the river. You keep yours open too."

Steve dropped a hand on the wiry little Pete's shoulder. "In the service I rode with men I considered good comrades, Pete. But none were ever as good and faithful as you and Bueno. No, I haven't forgotten Mister Blake Ollinger. I'll keep my eyes open."

Others, it seemed, were thinking about Ollinger too. The last night out from the river Race and Lynn Ellison came up to

Steve's fire. Lynn's serene cheerfulness was missing; she was sober and thoughtful. Race spoke gravely.

"I don't know what's become of Ollinger, Steve. I hope he's headed for the ends of the earth. In case he isn't, you let me handle him. He's my responsibility."

Steve thought of that derringer he'd seen Ollinger handle with such unerring dexterity and deadliness that morning, so far away now, when the *Spartan* was ready to pull away from the landing at Yuma. The desert had toughened Race Ellison amazingly, but Race was fundamentally a wagon man, and the way of men with guns was a secondary thing with him.

"Ollinger," said Steve, "is the responsibility of any man he tries to throw a gun on. If that man is me — well — we'll see."

Lynn lingered when Race went away. "For the first time since leaving Fort Staley I'm afraid again," she said simply.

"Now, now," chided Steve gently, "after that Apache attack I thought you'd never know fear again, Lynn."

"For myself — yes. For others — no. Race and — and you, Steve. You'll be — very careful?"

He smiled down at her. "Watch me."

They saw Calumet in the late afternoon,

and they saw the river beyond, with the sinking sun striking up a coppery glitter across the turgid, silt-laden waters. The breath of it came up to them, and this big, mean devil of waters seemed to leer at them.

To Lynn, as they looked at it, Steve said, "It's got the history of the ages in it and it will always be a surly, hungry brute. But it makes a big chunk of the continent live. And men will always find a way to use it and whip it. Somehow, if it wasn't exactly like it is, it wouldn't be right."

They set up their wagon camp along the flats above town. In a lower meadow the Overgaard and Fallon wagons still stood, and there were mules in the corrals with men tending them. A merchant from town, a broad and stocky man named Coulter, sought out Steve Cloud and Race Ellison and had his say.

"I've been keeping an eye on those wagons and seeing to it that the mules were cared for. Not because I loved Overgaard and Fallon, but because somebody had to take care of a valuable property. I know Hack Overgaard is dead. What about Grimes Fallon?"

They told him the story, all of it. Coulter, an honest and practical man, shrugged. "If they wanted to play the game that way, they can't kick at the results. Don't blame you for what you did. It was your only way out. And as I say, Fallon and Overgaard wrote the rules. Question is, what now? Fallon and Overgaard may have kin somewhere I can contact, but that could be a long-drawn-out business. You got anything to suggest?"

"I anticipate needing more wagons and more mules on my next trip to Staley," said Race. "I'd be willing to take over some of those wagons and mules at a fair price."

"Why not take 'em all?" suggested Coulter. "You need more money, come to me. Your first trip to Staley has done something. It's opened up new country. People will start moving out that way. A smart man in this country considers the future. I'm willing to gamble on that future. For my share of the money I might even consider a minor partnership, Ellison. Think on it and let me know. You need settled establishment at this end of the trail and I can provide that. Yeah, think on it."

Race did, quickly, and it made sense. He would need a warehouse here at Calumet. This thing could grow big, very big. Not only for army supplies but for civilian needs too. And this man named Coulter had roots already set along that line.

"I like the idea, Coulter. I'll see you tonight to talk it over. The money for those wagons and mules, we can hold it pending contact with Overgaard or Fallon kin. Then we'll pay it over. That's as square a shake as can be arranged."

"Suits you, suits me," said Coulter. "See you tonight."

He went away, and Race turned to Steve. "There's a partnership for you, too, Steve. I'd already decided on that."

Steve shook his head. "Thanks, but no, Race. Oh, I'll be taking out your wagon trains for some time yet. But once the Apache threat is wholly gone from the country along the trail, I got my sights set on a ranch up among the piñons. I'll let you know when the time comes. That Coulter — I like him. He's a good man, Race. You'll be smart to tie in with him."

Calumet at night. Even in the relatively short time they'd been away from it, it had grown a little. The tide of human expansion across the frontier was quickening, flowing higher all the time. It was a tide that would never stop flowing until the final limits of the country were reached. And then the waters would deepen. A smart man calculated his future accordingly.

Steve spent an hour in town, doing

nothing in particular. Pete Orrick and Bueno scouted mysteriously then sought Steve out. "He was here yesterday," reported Pete. "But he took a horse an' rode out last night, down river. Could be his nerve ran out, boy. Maybe we've seen the last of Blake Ollinger."

Steve went back to the wagon camp. He was surprised when Lynn Ellison came up out of the dark. "Thought you'd be in town with Race," said Steve.

She shook her head. "Trail life has spoiled me, I guess. I can't think of anything Calumet could offer me better than the comforts of my own wagon. Come walk with me."

They went on past the wagons, resting huge and awkward in the dark. A wagon, mused Steve, was only alive when it was rolling. . . . They passed the corrals and heard the mules chomping hungrily as they fed, and smelled the warm, animal odor of them. Then all this was behind them and there was only the open meadows and the river, the surly old river, sliding along under the stars.

"That high country — that piñon country of yours, Stephen — you must show it to me some time," said Lynn. "The picture of it has been in my mind ever since you first spoke of it."

"Next trip out," promised Steve. "We'll ride up there, if the trail seems open enough to me. We'll — !"

He broke off, and all the wariness he had ever possessed leaped up in one hard, bright blaze. For there was a figure there ahead of them — not twenty steps distant, a figure Steve instantly knew. Blake Ollinger!

Ollinger' s voice had a wild, ragged note in it. "Waiting for this chance, Cloud! Some things I'm never satisfied to leave along my back trail — like a man still alive who's done me dirt. I knew you were about due to arrive. So I rode out last night, and this morning located your dust and watched you come in. And I've watched you since and so — here we are and now we settle!"

Lynn was at Steve's left. His left hand settled on her slim shoulder, then straightened with a force that threw her away and to the ground. And his right hand was dragging at the gun at his hip!

The reports of Blake Ollinger's favorite derringer were small and sharp and spiteful against the spread of the river and the meadows. But the bellow of Steve Cloud's heavy Colt gun sent the echoes rocketing and held a strange and smashing finality.

Steve felt the burn of a derringer bullet along the outer round of his shoulder and felt the breath of another past his face. But for Blake Ollinger it was a lethal, solid blow in the center of the chest, a blow that drove him back and left him hanging on his heels.

Steve shot again, holding lower. Ollinger's gasp held a thin, whistling sound in it. Then he jackknifed at the waist and never felt the earth when it struck his face.

For a long second Steve waited and watched. Then he whirled.

"Lynn!"

She came up out of the earth's shadow, and his arms went around her. "Girl — I had to do it — get you out of the way. I didn't mean to hurt — !"

She sealed his lips with a soft palm. "Hold me, Stephen — just hold me! I'm not hurt. Oh — my dearest — my dearest — ! There'll never be fear again. Oh, Stephen — hold me — !"

Her hand at his lips dropped and her own lips took its place. The circle of his arms grew tighter. And the old river rolled and the old desert waited under the stars. And if time moved it didn't count at all. . . .